SEVIL BÜTÜNER was born on an autumn day, her favourite season of the year, in Izmir, Turkey. She is married with two children. Her daily routine includes nature walks and doing yoga, while her hobbies include listening to classical and jazz music, and watching and spending time with animals. Residing half of each year in her home in Salford, England, you could most likely catch her at a nearby park. Described by her friends and family as a lover of dogs, birds and squirrels, she always has a few treats in her bag to give them.

When she was diagnosed with breast cancer in 2013, she felt that this was a warning sign for her to change and revaluate things. This led her to an inward journey, which rekindled her passion for writing that was buried deep for many years.

According to Sevil, who loves writing and reading fiction, every story introduces its readers to different worlds and offers the chance to reside in them for a while. The moments in which she is most at peace are the ones where she is able to write down her thoughts, with her steaming cup of coffee, watching the rain outside. Spiritualism and healing have fascinated her throughout her life. She believes that wandering in the depths of one's mind is a magical journey filled with miracles, and writing is the best way to begin. 'It's never too late for new beginnings,' the writer always says, publishing her first novel at the age of fifty. She is the author of a children's book published in Turkey, and many of her short stories were published in an esteemed literary magazine.

WHISPERS
OF
A FAIRY

Sevil Bütüner

The Book Guild Ltd

First published in Great Britain in 2022 by
The Book Guild Ltd
Unit E2 Airfield Business Park,
Harrison Road, Market Harborough,
Leicestershire. LE16 7UL
Tel: 0116 2792299
www.bookguild.co.uk
Email: info@bookguild.co.uk
Twitter: @bookguild

Typeset in 11pt Adobe Jenson Pro

Printed and bound in the UK by TJ Books LTD, Padstow, Cornwall

ISBN 978 1914471 407

British Library Cataloguing in Publication Data.
A catalogue record for this book is available from the British Library.

MIX
Paper from
responsible sources
FSC® C013056

In loving memory of my father,
You are still with us, I can feel your presence…

Chapter 1

AFTER THE DEATH OF HER FATHER BARD, MELISSA HAD mourned for a long time; she had felt as if a piece of her was now missing. Bard had been her closest friend for as long as her life. They could understand each other without words. Their perspectives on life, their views, the things that made them tick, the things that they enjoyed – the two were similar in almost every aspect. Bard supported, trusted and stood behind Melissa through everything. They couldn't get enough of each other's conversations. On long winter nights, those chats they had, in front of the fireplace with a cup of hot chocolate in both of their hands, were never to be forgotten. There were only two matters with the mention of which their conversations halted and the strong bond between them wilted: Bard's youth in Scotland and music. It was as if his life had begun at eighteen, upon this land in America. There was no mention of anything prior. Whenever these topics were raised, his gaze would darken and deepen like a bottomless well, and this calm and composed person would turn into an angry, bitter man.

She had been in fourth grade in elementary school when Melissa had understood the severity of the situation. Their music teacher had announced in the parent-teacher meeting that 'all children shall learn to play the flute' and required the parents' assistance in the matter. Bard had waited for the meeting to end and everyone to be dispersed; after that, he approached the teacher to say that he didn't want Melissa to participate in the activity. When the teacher perseveringly tried to explain that this was necessary for the children's development, he only got more furious; so, with a louder and more stern tone he said, "I

1

absolutely forbid it – music will have no place in my daughter's life." His crimson-red face and his fierce gaze had shocked and terrified Melissa as well as her teacher.

Thus, for Melissa, music had also become a taboo, just like Scotland; she had no choice but to bury these two things deep within the depths of her curiosity. That was, of course, until Bard had mentioned them in the last days of his life…

How she would wish that her father was still alive; all the melodies were still silent, and the past was still there in the dark depths of their minds clouded in its usual mystery. Time did nothing to help the pain; his absence hurt more and more with each day; the black hole in her heart grew ever more. She had not just lost her father; she had lost her companion, her closest friend and her biggest fan.

Although Melissa's relationship with her father was truly special, she was also very fond of her mother Judith. After Bard's unexpected departure, the bond between mother and daughter had grown even fonder. She made sure that her mother did not fall into loneliness. This year had been tough for both of them; they were thoroughly shaken and their world had crumbled apart.

Judith's only support in life was her daughter Melissa; she now had no one else left. Still, Judith never wanted her daughter to put her own life on hold to be there for her – that's why she always warned Melissa about not neglecting her own private life and her fiancé, to which Melissa often jokingly replied by saying, "I can keep up with all of you." Although frankly, she did not feel this way deep down most of the time. She often caught herself questioning the place of her fiancé Ron in her life, just like she did now.

Ron had just left. Melissa had half an hour to have the bed all to herself. She closed her eyes in the hope that she could catch some more sleep, yet at that instance the images of last night flooded her imagination and she lost sleep. They had met up with Ron's colleagues for drinks. The conversation revolved around business and networking. They seemed to have forgotten that Melissa was also there. If Ron had shown some sensitivity and noticed it, then she wouldn't have minded their attitude or felt left out. This was not the first time as well, and she was starting to resent the situation. Not to mention, when she opened up to Ron about her feelings, he reprehended her by saying, "You are being too sensitive. It's not like you are making an effort to join in on the conversation – you are acting distant as well."

At times like this, which came around a bit too frequently, the cautionary words of her father, told from before he got ill, rang in her ears: "You're not happy with Ron; I can see it in your eyes."

Melissa averted her gaze as she replied, "That is not true, we're doing fine."

Bard had grabbed his daughter's face and turned it towards him: "I want you to think of your own happiness as much as he thinks of his own, honey."

Trying to shake off her thoughts, she tossed the duvet away, sat up and dangled her legs from the edge of the bed. She looked around as she fiddled with the white plush rug with her feet. She picked up the photo frame on the bedside table with Ron's smiling picture, and as she looked at the picture, she thought, *I have to be fair to him, he did reassure me a lot after my father's death.* However, he also was rushing to make sure that everything was back to normal and he seemed annoyed that Melissa's pain lingered on. According to Ron, death was just as natural as birth, and Melissa would be able to get over it in no time, if only she could perceive the situation as such. "Nonsense," she hissed through her teeth as she put the picture in place. Taking a deep breath, she stood, walked towards the window and opened the thick grey satin curtains – she always found these curtains too gloomy. The sunlight coming in immediately enlivened the bedroom. She thought the black and white decoration was displeasing. When she moved in with Ron, the furniture was new, so changing the décor was not an option. She had hung a few paintings on the white wall to add some colour. The huge nude oil painting above the black leather headboard of the bed was what Melissa liked the most about the room.

She went to the bathroom, washed her face and brushed her teeth, then looked fixedly into her moss-green eyes in the mirror for a while, as if to dive deep into the mysteries of her own soul, trying to find something there, to see beyond the visible. She asked, "What do you really want?" Although, she already knew the answer...

She went back into the room and opened the mirrored door on the right side of the closet which belonged to her; she chose randomly from a pile of clothes that were mostly trousers, jumpers and T-shirts. Wardrobe layout was another issue she had quarrelled about with Ron. Ron criticised her, saying, "How do you never get bothered by this mess?" And Melissa defended herself by enquiring back, "Don't you ever get tired of trying to be so orderly all the time?"

After getting dressed, she put on light makeup with eyeliner and mascara; she was ready to go out. She was going to spend her day off with her mother. She picked up two cat biscuits from the kitchen, locked the apartment door and quickly went down the two floors of stairs. When she opened the heavy red iron door of the building, she was met with the tabby cat waiting for her as usual. The kitty would greet her outside whenever she left the house. Melissa sat down on the step, handed it biscuits, stroked its head affectionately, then got going.

She didn't take the car; she wanted to walk. She used to walk a lot with her father. When she dwelled more on it, she began to fall back into that great emptiness again. Whatever this feeling was, its source could not just be the loss of her father; she thought that there must be other things coming up to the surface of her consciousness through the pain she felt about her father's death. Yes, it must have been that; this loss had surely created an impact like a great earthquake which upset the balance of her mind. Her life seemed to be a huge puzzle; there were so many missing pieces that it would not ever be clear unless she found them and put them in place.

Of course, one of the main sources of this confusion was her father's words on his deathbed. "Go to Scotland!" Why did he want something like this when he himself had only visited there once after Melissa was born, and he hadn't even let anyone talk about the place? At the moment, she had not known the answer; if her father saw it necessary, he must have had a sensible and significant reason. Maybe he'd wanted to help his daughter for the last time, had tried to guide her, as he always had throughout his life... Yes, Melissa was going to fulfil his request. She needed to get away and make this journey to clear her mind and clarify her thoughts. In the current phase of her life, she felt spiritually at a crossroads. She had the feeling that she was in the middle of an important transformation. It was impossible to stop now; she had to choose her direction and move forward. Thus, she had made her decision and chose to follow the path leading to Scotland. The key to her peace of mind was perhaps amongst the missing pieces of the puzzle in her father's mysterious past. She had to complete the puzzle.

As she wondered with her mind occupied by these thoughts, she had reached her mother's house unknowingly. The walk had done her good; she felt much livelier and more energetic. She was also greatly uplifted with the relief of having reached a decision.

The smell of cinnamon cookies fresh out of the oven enveloped Melissa when she reached the door. In the past, she used to be greeted by this very same fragrance when she came home from school. She wished to return to those days for a moment; how nice would it be if all three of them could be together again. She smiled, with happy memories flickering in her mind. She had once knocked over a tray of cookies that her mother had left to cool on the kitchen counter while playing catch with her father; all the cookies fell and scattered on the floor, all crumbled. Bard had swept away the mess quietly, then tried to make it up to his wife with a bunch of flowers from the garden. On one occasion, on Mother's Day, they did not let Judith into the kitchen as the father and daughter decided to cook a special meal for her together, of course, once again making a mess in the kitchen.

Judith lovingly embraced her daughter. She had her white-blonde hair tied around her neck as usual, and this style highlighted her large green eyes. She wore pearl earrings to match with her white polka-dot chiffon dress.

Melissa looked with admiration, smiling. "I'll never once see you casual and unkempt, will I?"

Judith poked Melissa on her nose affectionately. "How about you try a little bit harder yourself?"

Laughing, they went into the living room together. Melissa saw the newspaper sitting in its usual place on the table. It was right in front of Bard's dark blue and purple plaid seat. Judith was still placing it there, as if Bard was going to come along again. Melissa gazed at it with a tingle in her heart, thinking how much her mother must be missing him; and when their eyes met, Judith tilted her head and pursed her lips.

"A habit of thirty years."

She was sitting on her husband's chair and was mindlessly stroking the armrests on which she had placed her hands. Sitting on the chair across from her – it was the same model, only patternless and khaki-coloured – Melissa looked around and reflected that she had always loved this place. The armchairs in which they were sitting now and the brick-lined fireplace were silent witnesses of the countless delightful conversations they'd had with her father.

Melissa got up and looked at the photos above the fireplace. On one side, there was her graduation photo with the three of them posing together. She touched it lightly with her index finger. How their eyes glimmered with joy and pride... On the other side, there was the photo of her dog, Dodo, licking her face. She took the frame and gazed at it with a smile.

"How old was I when this photo was taken; six or seven, right?"

"You're six years old there, if I'm not mistaken."

Melissa talked with a childlike lilt to her voice. "Won't you tell me how you named him once again? I love hearing that story."

Judith had got lost in the photo in her hand as she pictured that day. "We searched a lot with your father to find out what breed we should get, as we wanted to have a friend that could get along well with children. When we decided to get a golden retriever, we got lucky, since after a little while one of our usual customers from the restaurant just came up to us and said that he wanted to adopt out a puppy."

A big smile spread across Judith's face as her gaze shifted back to the photo. "You had just started talking back then. When your father came in with the puppy in his arms, you shouted 'dodo, dodo' with glee, and that's what we named him."

Melissa sighed wistfully. "He was a very good, smart dog."

"He would know what time you got back from school; he would wait in front of the window."

"He brought so much joy to my life. I wish every child could grow up smothered by such unconditional love." Melissa pressed the photo to her chest and continued. "I remember the day he died; when I saw that he was sick in the morning and stroked his belly, I somehow knew he was dying, and you know, at that moment I decided to become a veterinarian."

Judith looked at her daughter with pride. Her reddish eyes glistened with tears. "Good thing you did – you are good at what you do. Your father was always very proud of you, just like I am. You know, he cried when I told him about your decision to become a vet."

"Ah... you never mentioned that."

Judith waved her hand around as if to dispel the heavy pathos that filled the air. "Let's drink our tea. The cookies must have cooled enough to eat by now."

While they were sipping their tea, Melissa took the opportunity to reveal her decision to go to Scotland. She explained at length and gave her reasons; her eyes flashed as she spoke, sometimes with tears welling up in the corners and sometimes with the bright glint of hope. Judith was listening tenderly. Although her daughter's sorrow pained her heart, she was happy to have raised such a sensitive, thoughtful and contemplative individual. When she finished speaking, her mother reached out to take Melissa's hand in both of her palms and caressed it. With a warm, loving smile, she said, "Come here," then she opened her arms and hugged her daughter.

Melissa was definitely in need of some encouragement. "What do you think? I should go, right?" she asked.

Judith stroked Melissa's hair. "I think you've made the right decision. If your father was alive, he would be happy that you responded to his request. This is about your future as much as it is about his past. I hope you find the answers you seek and need." She kissed her daughter's auburn head resting on her chest.

Her mother's arms were a safe haven, and now, as she delighted in the chance to take refuge there, she was grateful to have such a mother. She was feeling more peaceful than she ever had in a long time as she looked up and grasped her wrinkled soft cheeks.

"I love you – you know that, right?"

She leaned her head back on Judith's chest and for a while surrendered herself in the arms that made her feel secure and loved.

She needed all the energy she could muster; it was not going to be easy to talk to Ron about this matter. She was able to anticipate his reaction, more or less. It did worry her, but there was no escape; she couldn't delay it any longer. She was tired of all this pretence.

When Melissa left Judith's place, the rain had already started pouring. Melissa actually loved to walk in the rain, but it was almost four o'clock in the afternoon and she didn't want to be late, so she took a taxi and went straight home.

She placed the dish in the oven, hoping that delicious lasagne and a fine wine would unwind Ron before she revealed her big decision. She set the table and lit some candles. She heard the doorbell rang just when she was taking off her apron. It was great timing.

Ron was taken aback by the delicious scent coming from inside as she opened the door; his curiosity grew stronger when he saw the dining table. Melissa put the tray she had in her hands on the table and reached out to him.

"Welcome!" She placed a peck on his lips.

Ron was stunned. *She must have decided to shake off that gloom at last*, he thought, rejoiced and relieved. He took off his jacket and hung it on the coat hanger at the entrance. "Ooh! To what do we owe this feast?" he exclaimed, loosening his tie.

His question hung in the air, as Melissa was just making her way to the CD player at that moment. She chose light jazz music. This was a new habit to her. She was just discovering the impact of music on human psychology. She could not understand why her father shut out something that could touch the human soul so brilliantly.

She turned back to head to the table. As soon as she jumped over the sand-coloured triple sofa, she met Ron's reprimanding gaze. Her cheeks flushed when she remembered that this move was on the list of things that Ron did not like her doing in the house; she straightened up the cushions in a hurry.

They ate their dinner, chit-chatting about usual daily matters. Melissa was waiting for the right moment to bring up the subject. She kept curling the red strand of hair on her finger, which fell persistently on her cheek. She did this unconsciously whenever she was nervous. If she had her mother or her father sitting opposite her right now, they would have immediately understood that something was wrong, but Ron had not yet discovered this pattern in her behaviour. This was unknown to him, as were many others...

She handed her glass to Ron. "Could you please pour me another glass of wine?"

Ron raised an eyebrow as he handed back the filled glass, enquiry clouding his hazel eyes. "You don't usually drink more than a glass – is there something wrong or is this a celebration?"

Melissa closed her eyes and took a deep breath. Thoughts and words swirled in her mind as she spun the glass in her palms.

"I don't know if it's good or bad, but I made a decision. The words my father said before his death haunt me; I plan to go to Scotland to understand what he was trying to tell me, why he directed me there and to solve the mystery in his past."

Melissa said all this in a snap, without looking at Ron's face, her eyes still closed. She would not have been able to say what she had just said if she had her eyes open. Ron was peering at her with a squinted, contemptuous gaze; he seemed as if he was trying to digest this unexpected development. "So, I assume you're still mourning then." His jaw tightened with anger; he was clenching his teeth so hard that the little shifts in the bones at his temples were visible. He spoke in a stern, sarcastic manner as Melissa watched him carefully across the table, as if she was watching a hand grenade without a pin.

"How long do you plan to stay?"

"I don't know yet. I guess until I find answers to my questions."

"If he wanted you to have the answers, he would have told you sooner. I think you're obsessing over this for no reason."

"This is what he uttered to me on his deathbed, Ron." Melissa spoke with a soft voice.

"Why is it so important to you to dig so deep into the past? What's the problem?"

The contempt in his tone was something that Melissa had never experienced with anyone else before; she thought it repulsed her. She leaned back on the chair and crossed her arms over her chest. Her determination was reflected in her gaze.

"This was my father's last request. I will pay him due respect and do whatever is necessary to honour his request, and I expect the same consideration from you."

The unease grew around the table and the tension became palpable with all its intensity. Although Melissa was worried for a moment, thinking whether she was in the wrong, she quickly dismissed the thought. No, she would no longer be the one who retreated, kept on his right side and accepted it all; there was nothing wrong with her demands and she would stand by them until the end. The straightness of her posture, the sharpness of her gaze, the determination in her expression were an unfamiliar sight to Ron. He was startled as well as surprised. His piercing gaze gradually gave way to anxiety, and his words started to sound like childish threats.

"I hope you don't expect me to come with you – I have a lot of work here." He shifted back slightly in his chair, his arms folded. "I don't approve of you going either."

Melissa was shocked by the realisation that she had been seeing Ron through a curtain of affection all this time; she could not believe how the man she was now seeing with the curtains open was so incredibly different then the man she knew before.

"Can you tell me why you don't approve?"

By what right did this man consider himself as the authority of approval? Her face flushed with anger and her chest tightened.

Ron shrugged. "I don't like being alone."

Melissa looked with pity as she watched this man sitting across from her, whom she knew to be serious and dignified, acting like an immature child. Her lips curled in a weary, scornful smile.

"Ron, the world does not revolve around you; this is about me and my dad. Won't you stop thinking about yourself for a change? I do not expect or even want you to come. I have to make this journey for my well-being, in order to gain some direction in my life."

Melissa knew that her efforts to express herself were futile. Her remarks lingered in the air, not reaching the person they were directed at.

Ron glanced at Melissa for a while then threw his napkin on the table. "I didn't know the life we have together made you so unhappy. I'm sorry for having this ridiculous idea that we would plan our future together."

As soon as he was done speaking, he got up. Melissa had her elbows on the table, rubbing her forehead and temples with both hands, hoping to find a way to express her distress. But with each passing minute, she was losing hope.

Her voice lowered into a whisper, reflecting her desperation and disappointment. "You don't understand, what I'm trying to say is…" Her voice trembled; there was a knot in her throat, but she did not want to cry or seem weak. She took a deep breath and gulped. Her mournful eyes did not reach Ron's gaze. "If you consider it calmly—"

Ron interrupted Melissa by lifting his hand up in a gesture to stop her. His gaze was freezing cold. "There's nothing to consider. Either you're with me or you are not; it's that simple. I can't just stand here and wait for you to make a decision; you must decide now."

He turned and walked towards the window. The rigidity of his thoughts was reflected in his stance. He stood there like a rock, looking out the window with his hands in his pockets.

This was what Melissa feared. Still, she had to admit that she didn't expect such a big reaction. There was only one thing she could do. She removed the ring from her finger and put it on the table as the tears gently moved past her eyelashes and poured down her cheeks, leaving wet trails on her freckled face.

"Once your anger subsides, you'll understand why I had to do this." She waited in vain for an answer. "Goodbye. I will drop by as soon as possible to collect my stuff."

When she got to her car, she hurled herself in, grasped the steering wheel tightly and started sobbing as she tried to control her trembling body. The tears slightly eased the stinging pain of resentment and calmed her. She checked her face in the sun visor's mirror, wiped away the mascara stains, wiped her nose, took a deep breath, then started the car and drove away.

She drove aimlessly for an hour, not knowing where she was heading. Each turn she took led her to a new path, just like in life. A page was turned in Melissa's life this evening, but she knew that life consisted of many more blank pages that she could fill to her heart's desires. She was going to be the author of her own story now. A strange sense of peace and relief took over her. She never knew she would feel this way.

When she finally arrived at her destination and parked her car, Judith opened the door right away, before she could ring the doorbell, and hugged her daughter.

"I saw the car approaching through the window. I was waiting for you tonight. I'm glad you're here. Come on, let's have some hot chocolate."

Their moss-green gazes read each other without the need for words. Melissa sat on the large sofa, pulled her legs up to her chest, rested her head on her knees and looked at her mother.

"Ron and I are done…"

Judith stroked her daughter's head as she lovingly regarded her. "Are you okay?"

Melissa lifted her head and straightened her back. "I will be."

They sat there, drinking their hot chocolate in silence. When Melissa finally eased off and felt sleepy, she curled up on her bed without changing into her pyjamas. Judith tucked her in and whispered, "I love you, honey." She then turned off the light and left her alone.

Chapter 2

IT WAS A BUSY DAY AT THE HAPPY PAWS CLINIC; APART FROM the appointments of usual patients, there were many emergency cases. The loud barks of the dogs in the clinic scared the poor kittens, who scurried to the safety of their owners' laps. The situation was not much different than any hospital emergency room, the only difference being that the patients were animals rather than humans.

After taking care of three patients one after the other, Melissa let her secretary know that she was going on a coffee break, then she plonked herself on the comfortable soft grey sofa in the private lounge room. She closed her eyes and loosened her muscles, drawing soft and deep breaths. She had been working here for four years now. She was the clinic's most popular veterinarian. Although there were two other veterinarians available, her appointment slots would usually fill up first. This was possibly because her job felt like a hobby to her; she took pleasure in doing what she did and was able to communicate with the animals, as well as with their owner, with ease. She'd felt that she had a special connection with animals ever since she was little; she even thought they understood her when she spoke to them. During their examination, most animals just stood calmly and let her do her job, which helped her be exceptionally accurate and quick with her diagnoses.

The ringing phone gave her a jolt; it was her secretary calling. "I'm afraid you'll have to get back to work, there is an emergency patient."

"Alright, okay, I'll be there immediately. I'm not sure what exactly is happening today, there are so many emergency cases coming in, aren't there?"

She went down to the reception to receive the documents of the patient. As she was gathering her red curly hair into a bun on top of her head and securing it with the pen in her hand, she saw Susan, one of the other veterinarians. Melissa whispered to her with a smile, "I don't think I'll be able to get out of bed tomorrow; I'm spent."

Susan tapped her with the back of her hand. "Hey! You didn't forget about tomorrow night, did you?"

Feigning an expression of sadness, Melissa fluttered the red lashes framing her moss-coloured eyes: "Oh no, you crushed my dreams of lying in bed all day."

Susan was Ron's cousin and she'd arranged for them to meet. At the time, everyone around Melissa was constantly setting her up with someone and Melissa was quite fed up with it; Susan, however, tried a different tactic and invited Ron to the clinic, thus not giving Melissa the chance to squirm out of it.

Ronald – everyone called him Ron – had just arrived in the city as a credit administration director for a bank. He was a successful, charismatic man who oozed confidence in his every move. He was also tall and very attractive with brown hair, hazel eyes and a good sense of style. He was an eligible bachelor. Although he was in his forties, he had yet to find that special someone he was looking for. That's exactly why Susan had introduced them to each other. With Melissa's talent of being able to communicate with everyone easily, Susan thought the two might have a chance.

For their first dinner date, Ron had chosen a cosy little restaurant and came to pick her up with a colourful bunch of peonies. He had opened her door as she got into the car, acting before the waiter in the restaurant to pull her chair for her. In short, he acted like a gentleman through and through.

After a few dates, Melissa thought, *I think I've found the person I was looking for*. She introduced Ron to her parents after four months of dating. They all got together for a late lunch on a Sunday. Judith and Bard had arrived early to the restaurant. It was a restaurant Bard formerly owned and had handed over. They wanted to choose a place that was meaningful and significant for the occasion.

Her parents got up to greet the couple as soon as they arrived and gave their daughter a hug. Judith leaned towards to hug Ron as well, but he resorted to just giving her a nod.

"It's nice to meet you."

Judith found his attitude peculiar, but she didn't want to form an opinion prematurely. *Maybe he's a bit too shy,* she thought. When the waiter came to take their order, they were all studying the menu in their hands. Bard and Judith chose to have Mexican chicken, while Melissa smiled and handed the menu to the waiter, saying, "I'll have the lasagne, please."

"I want a Caesar salad," said Ron.

After the waiter collected their menus and left, Ron pointed towards Melissa. "I am careful about my diet; I try to avoid the unhealthy, high-calorie, fatty foods, unlike some others. I do try to warn her constantly but…"

Melissa blushed slightly; squinting her eyes, she put on a fake smile. "Thank you for looking after my health, you are so kind."

Bard felt no need to hide the anger in his voice. "I am quite sure that my daughter knows much about eating and staying healthy, more than many people, I might say, though it is certainly okay to pamper yourself from time to time."

Although Judith was also annoyed, she decided to change the subject as she sensed the tension in the air and asked Ron about his family and work.

While waiting for their coffee after the meal, Ron looked around then turned to Bard. "Melissa said this place was yours before."

"Yes, it was. I've spent forty years of my life here and I handed it over to good hands; it's time to rest now."

When Bard was done speaking, he glanced around the place with a soulful yet proud look. The wooden table in front of the window, where he'd sat with the Crowns on his first day when he'd come here for a job application, was still in its same place. *One of the turning points in my life,* he thought. It was an intimate, small family restaurant and its customers were mostly regulars. With Ron's question, Bard's attention shifted back to their table. "Did you decide to quit due to economic reasons? Was it not a profitable business?"

Bard laughed out loud. "It is clear that you are a banker! No, no, it had nothing to do with money. It was demanding, tiring work." She hugged Judith and kissed her cheek. "I also wanted to spend more time with my lovely wife."

Although the first meeting with the family was a bit formal and even a bit tense at first, overall it went well. As they said their goodbyes, Melissa's parents were cautious about keeping their distance this time. They were a bit bothered by his refusal to shake hands and his controlling manner; still, they did not think that he was too bad in general. Bard did not feel at ease, but for now, he didn't want to share his feelings about Ron with Melissa.

It was a Friday and, as per tradition, Melissa was going to meet Ron at their favourite restaurant that they always went to. After work, she went straight to the house, took a shower and wore a green dress with a deep open back plunge which complimented her moss-green eyes. She developed a keenness for wearing dresses after she started dating Ron, as he liked to dress up to dine in luxury restaurants. She wore some eyeliner and mascara, then finished off with a peach-coloured lipstick. She did a messy updo; it was impossible to tame her wild red curls anyway. She then put on her black heels and checked herself in the mirror. She was happy with her reflection in the mirror; she smiled and thought of Judith. Her mother often complained, saying, "If only you got rid of those jeans and put on something more feminine once in a while, you would have already got married and have given me grandchildren." She thought that a woman should be married before she turned thirty.

Ron was waiting when Melissa got to the restaurant. He got up and greeted her, gave her a tiny kiss on the lips, and pulled out her chair for her. Ron held Melissa's hand with both hands and gazed at her lovingly, then took her hand to his lips and kissed gently. "You look gorgeous," he said. Melissa smiled bright.

Throughout the meal, they talked about current events and goings-on at work. When the waiter brought the dessert menu, Melissa placed her hands on her stomach. "I'm so full, I can't have a bite more."

Ron insisted, his hazel eyes sparkling with a mischievous glint. "Let's just share a portion."

The waiter put a dessert tray with an elegant curved lid on the table. At Ron's sign, he lifted the lid and walked back. A ring box was at the middle of the tray. Ron opened the box and presented it to Melissa. "Will you marry me and be my wife?"

Melissa put her hands over her agape mouth, her eyes locked on the ring; she was stunned by his surprise.

"So, are you going to give me an answer?" he asked, upon which Melissa recovered with a happy laugh.

"Yes, of course, yes!"

Ron put the ring on Melissa's finger and kissed her hand with the ring on as he said, "I want you to move in with me now." The people sitting at the nearby tables applauded and cheered for them.

They hosted a small engagement dinner two weeks later, with only their families attending. Bard and Judith thought the decision of the young couple was a bit hurried, but they kept it to themselves and joined in on their daughter's excitement and joy. Judith couldn't help thinking, *Did I put too much pressure on her to find someone proper and get married soon?* Whereas Bard desperately hoped that he was wrong in his intuition about Ron.

Melissa had lived by herself for years, and it was hard at first to share a home with someone. Besides, Ron's meticulousness and obsession with order didn't make it any easier.

Even after more than a year of being together, this was still an issue for them.

Melissa had just come home from work; she was rubbing her hands together under the running water, washing her hands in agitation with tears running down her cheeks. *This must be some kind of a disorder; I am reaching out to hug and kiss him, and he pushes me aside, bothered by the little speck of dust he sees on me; what kind of a man is this?*

When she went into the bedroom and opened the door to change her clothes, her favourite dress caught her eyes and she remembered that night.

It was a Saturday. There was a gathering hosted by the bank for the top executives. Melissa had gone to the hairdresser and had her hair done. She felt so beautiful, dressed in a pleated chiffon tie-neck dress with an open back and a flared high skirt.

Ron came out of the bathroom, glanced at Melissa and pointed at her dress. "Honey, you're not thinking about wearing that, are you?"

"I've actually worn it, haven't I? What's wrong with it?"

Ron kissed her cheek as Melissa checked her dress. "You look beautiful, but you have to wear something more formal." He probed around the closet and pulled out a black dress. "Like this, for instance."

Melissa shrugged, took what Ron was showing her and put it on. She felt utterly resentful, but as always, she chose not to show it. "Well, it is your party, after all…"

Melissa shook off her thoughts and came back to her senses. She put on something comfy, trying to sympathise, thinking, *What else to do but to accept him for who he is?* After all, they did usually get along, didn't they?

Chapter 3

Bard, 2015

BARD HAD LEFT TOBERMORY AFTER GRADUATING FROM high school. Tobermory was a small city on the Isle of Mull in Scotland. Why he left was a complete mystery. He had only returned briefly when he found out that his father was seriously ill. His friend Sean had called and told him that this might be the last chance he got to see his father, so he had to go.

Bard was not at all prepared for what he encountered when he arrived at the hospital. His father was frail like a twig. He looked small and defenceless like a baby in his sickbed. His heart ached as he was wrapped in an incredible sense of guilt. He had never thought of the man who gave life to him while he was busy getting away from his own fears. He had wasted all those good times they could have had and now he was praying that they may have a little more. Richard held on for three days. The only thing that comforted Bard was that his father knew that he was coming and was with him in his last days. Except for the funeral and the ceremony attended by a few people, he didn't see anyone; even with Sean, he spoke only briefly. He left the country quickly soon after as if he was running away.

Bard had been blessed with good luck after he came to America at the age of eighteen. He thought that his wife Judith was one of the best things to ever happen to him, and he was grateful for it. He knew that he owed all his achievements in his business and his social life to having such an understanding, supportive woman like her in his life. In the first years of their relationship and marriage, despite aching to share his past with his wife, he just couldn't bring himself to tell her everything. He had buried those days deep in his memory. There was a barrier that he couldn't surpass; it was not easy to break down those walls. What good would that do anyway? After all, Judith loved and accepted him as he was; there was no need to open old wounds when everything was already fine. Life for the two of them began when they met, and they were happy together for thirty years.

~

Bard had been feeling a little tired lately, and he had lost his appetite slightly. Winter was over; the seasons were changing. He did not pay it any attention, thinking that it must have been the spring fatigue. He had a sensitive stomach; he did suffer from it from time to time. There was no point in telling Judith and Melissa and worrying them. He decided to wait for a while and go to the doctor if it didn't go away. These days he had other things on his mind than his health anyhow: he was worried for his daughter; he had to voice his concern even though it might make her angry.

On Sunday, as she walked towards the park to meet with her father, Melissa was pondering: *We often used to go on strolls together and chat – how nice that was. I wish I could make more time for those now.* She smiled and waved upon seeing him. She kissed him on the cheek when she reached up to him and took his arm; they wandered into the park together.

Spring was bursting in full bloom. The youthful light green leaves of the trees were swaying in harmony with the gentle breeze of the wind; the birds chirped around, joining in on the festivities. This path, with the trees lining up on both sides and the wrought-iron streetlights and benches, always felt quite magical to Melissa; she often imagined that there would be a beautiful fairy-tale castle at the end. For a while, they walked arm in arm and chatted about this or that casually. Melissa fed the squirrels with the pack of nuts she brought with her. They chuckled remembering how she used to go running behind the animals, screaming to hold and pet them. However, Bard suddenly grew serious.

"You were a happy, joyful child."

Melissa flashed a wide smile. "I still am!"

They arrived near the pond in the meantime; Bard pointed to the wooden bench under a great plane tree. "Let's sit there."

The pond swarmed with ducks, swans and seagulls. They were all alive with the coming of the spring; nature was in a rush to reproduce and proliferate. Some were fussing and fretting to protect their offspring while others were carrying brushwood in their little beaks to make their nests. They watched children trying to feed the animals with a smile on their faces. They both enjoyed being in touch with nature and observing the life bustling all around them. They sat hand in hand in silence for a while.

Bard was first to break the silence. "I don't think you're happy with Ron."

Melissa didn't expect to hear that; she looked at him in bewilderment. "Daddy!"

Bard lifted his head to the sky, drew a deep breath and turned to face Melissa as he exhaled. "Just hear what I have to say. The rest is up to you. I feel that it is my duty to warn you. You are more precious to me than anything else in the world and I don't ever want to see you upset."

Melissa still wasn't sure where this conversation was going to go. She continued listening to him with curiosity.

"Ron may be a nice guy, but he's not the guy for you. He's not looking for a companion for life; he's looking for someone who would make a good wife for him and he's trying to mould you into that role." He gently tugged the curl that fell on his daughter's cheek behind her ear and continued with a compassionate expression: "My dear, you're so special, I don't think you're fit for that role. Being an accessory in someone else's life will only dull your shine. I remember you being the light of every room you entered, but now with great sorrow I see that your light is dwindling. Your eyes don't look the same. What I want is your happiness only, and that can only be possible if you are true to who you really are in your heart."

Bard kissed her on the forehead. "You don't have to say anything now – just promise me that you'll think about it."

Tears rolled down her eyes as Melissa embraced her father tightly. "I promise, I will not let anyone change me."

Bard added, after looking away sadly, "And anything…" A determined expression was cast over his face. "Soon I will tell you about Scotland and my past there – there are things you should know. But this is enough sombreness for one day."

Melissa was excited to hear that. This was the first time that her father had ever even brought the issue up. What a surprise this was!

"Then you should promise as well. You'll tell me soon, don't you forget!"

"As soon as possible."

They sat there for a while, arm in arm, enjoying the blissful confidence and peace of having each other by their side.

Bard had decided to talk about his past after witnessing Melissa examining a dog at her clinic recently. The dog was moaning; he was suffering greatly from a tumour. Melissa was talking to the poor dog as she caressed its little face. After only a while, the dog's moans silenced, and he was soothed as if there was something magical in his daughter's touch… What he saw made Bard question, could it be that she too…? He had to tell her what he knew before it was too late…

~

Bard was awakened by a dream that he hadn't had for forty-seven years. After all those years, he'd had it again! Only with a slight difference… The fairy was calling out to him with her sweet mystical melody. He woke up covered in sweat. He tried to sleep again, repeating to himself that it was just a nightmare, but it was almost morning and he couldn't fall asleep. He got out the bed so as not to disturb Judith by tossing and turning constantly. Today, his stomach was even worse; he went to the kitchen to brew some tea. He was just thinking, *I should go see a doctor soon*, when a sharp pain took the breath out of his lungs. The shooting pain, which started in his stomach, travelled to his chin and spread to his arm. It was so excruciating that his eyes lost sight and his legs went weak. Just then, he understood that this agony was not to do with his stomach but his heart. Beads of cold sweat dripped from his forehead; the world, his surroundings, everything around him started to slip away from him. He was watching, feeling life leaving his body like he was watching a slow-motion movie, but there was nothing he could do to stop the tape from rolling. With the second jab of that shooting he curled up on the stone floor of the kitchen and went numb.

Melissa was treating the first patient that morning, a dog with a leg injury. She shivered for a moment when the phone in the examination room rang; she felt her heart sink and the air get heavier in her lungs as if she was being choked by the force of an invisible hand. They would never have connected the call to the phone here if it wasn't important. She let her assistant take over her patient and responded to the call anxiously. From in between her mother's sobs, she was able to pick out the words 'hospital' and 'your father'. She immediately left work. The roads seemed never-ending; she felt like she had to drive for hours before she finally made it to the hospital. She found her mother waiting in front of the intensive care unit. Her face was sheet white; her fearful eyes were swollen from crying; she was clutching her jacket in between her arms. She tried to explain everything to her daughter as they hugged each other and cried. Bard had had a heart attack and was in a coma, the doctors said.

Melissa's whole body gave into tremors with the impact of the devastating news. The white walls of the hospital resembled walls of ice. She felt as if she was trapped in an avalanche, waiting desperately to hear something good and hopeful, to feel the warmness of glad tidings. They sat down together, still clasping each other, trying to console and reassure each other.

Melissa squeezed her mother's hand firmly. "He'll be fine, he's a strong man."

She was trying not to lose hope. Every time the double doors of the intensive care unit swung open, they stirred to see if anyone was coming for them. Surges of hope and fear shifted in their souls. When finally a doctor came through the doors and approached them, the two women clasped their cold and shivering hands together. "Just tell us he's fine," Melissa kept muttering under her breath.

The doctor nodded to greet them; it was not possible to read anything from her expression. After seconds which felt like centuries, her words provided them with nothing more than a faint light in the darkness.

"Our patient is in stable condition. He had a severe heart attack – from what we know, this is probably the third one."

Judith broke in immediately; she was perplexed. "But this is the first time we are experiencing something like this."

Melissa intervened before the doctor could: "Sometimes, in fact, quite commonly, minor attacks can occur without being noticed at all; I'm guessing that's what happened with Dad." She introduced herself to the doctor and stated that she was a veterinarian.

"Yes," the doctor agreed, "your daughter is right. It is a common occurrence." She looked at the two women with compassion. "Let's try to get through today and tonight, we will make another evaluation tomorrow. Now you can come in and see him, but please keep it short."

The intensive care unit was quite large. The patients' beds were separated from each other by curtains. The nurses were regularly walking around, checking the data on the medical equipment that were connected to the patients. Seeing Bard in there was overwhelming for both of them. He was lying unconscious in the hospital bed surrounded by monitors and devices with an oxygen mask covering his mouth, the cables of an ECG machine on his chest, an IV tube attached to his arm and another cable attached to his other hand that connected to a monitor. His face was pale and lifeless. This should have been an environment that Melissa was accustomed to from her line of work, yet when it was a piece of her laying in front of her, it had an entirely different impact.

Judith grabbed Bard's hand and stroked his thinning ginger hair, then she leaned over his delicate, gentle face upon which she'd gazed with the same undying love for thirty-five years, and she kissed his rosy freckles, his brown eyes which still melted her heart after all these years and the subtle lines forming around those eyes… Never-ending tears rained down from her cheeks. Her shoulders had collapsed under the weight of her sorrow; she was having trouble standing straight. Melissa was devastated to see them in this state. *I must remain strong for both of them,* she thought, then held her mother by her shoulders and helped her walk.

"Come on, let's get out now."

She spoke with the nurse to find them a small empty room; with the promise that she would let her know if there were any developments, she convinced Judith to rest a little.

Melissa had collapsed on the sofa in the waiting room. She was sitting there completely still with her head tossed back and her eyes fixed on the ceiling. Was all that had just happened real? Her father was still quite young; he seemed quite healthy as well. It was just this Sunday when they wandered around in the park together. When she recalled their conversation, she suddenly realised that their conversation could have been a hint that Bard was indeed not feeling well: his words, his decision to mention his past... It could not be a coincidence.

"Oh, Dad! How different it would be if only you cared about yourself as much as you cared about me."

The realisation hurt Melissa; she cried until there were no tears left to cry.

In the next few hours, Bard seemed to regain consciousness slightly for two or three times. His eyelids trembled, his fingers wiggled and his cheeks gained some colour. At those moments, he deliriously called out a name that neither Melissa nor Judith had ever heard before: "Maidie." The women looked at each other in confusion. Who was this? Bard slipped back into unconsciousness before he could say anything more.

Melissa took Judith's hand and led her to the door. She informed the nurse that they were going to go down to the cafeteria, then urged her mum, "Let's go have a cup of coffee."

They sat at a table in the cafeteria away from the crowd. Judith was very quiet; her empty eyes wandered around as she played with her cup rather than drinking her coffee. The sorrow in his gaze was now accompanied by bitter indignation.

Melissa grabbed her mother's hand and squeezed it; their moss-green eyes stared at each other with a great understanding.

"It must be an old friend or a cousin from his past or else we would have known. He doesn't like bringing up his past, you know that."

Judith replied, forcing a smile, "Yes, you must be right." She then added, taking a deep breath in, straightening her shoulders and lifting her head, as if she had just come to a new decision, "I just want to see that he gets better, nothing else matters."

On his third day in the ICU, when Bard gazed at his wife with tired eyes and reached out to her, Judith grabbed his hands and placed them in her palms. Bard spoke with difficulty, in a low voice. "We lived a beautiful and a happy life with you." He closed his eyes, gathered his strength and continued. "I don't know where I would be without you."

He was out of breath and tired; his voice got lower and lower, so Judith moved closer to hear him. Bard continued, using all his energy to hold on to his wife's hand tightly. "Thank you," he said. "I love you." He was now thoroughly exhausted; no power was left in his frail body.

Judith was shaking and weeping. "I love you too, don't leave me, I cannot continue without you." She then placed her trembling finger over her husband's lips. "But hush now, don't tire yourself anymore."

The nurse also warned them that the patient needed rest and asked them to leave. Just when they were about to go, they heard Bard's voice. "Melissa!"

She turned back and leaned over him. "Yes, Dad, I'm here." Melissa glanced at the nurse anxiously; after receiving her silent approval, she continued. "Rest a little – you are very tired, we'll talk later."

Bard's mouth was dry; she could see that he hardly could muster the power to wet his dried lips in order to speak. "No, now, not later."

Despite his frailty, he sounded determined. He was trying to talk by uttering only single phrases like he was speaking in his sleep. The words 'talent', 'burden', 'music' were followed by other words, which Melissa could not make any sense of, like 'cave' and 'fairy'. Bard opened his eyes with his last effort; he quickly lost consciousness after uttering, "You may also have it, go to Scotland!"

In that last glance, Melissa realised the spark of life in her father's eyes was fading. The most important man in her life, her dearest, was slowly drifting away and there was nothing they could do to stop it.

Both were drained to their core as they were seated on the chairs at the waiting room. They did not have the strength even to seek out words to comfort one another. The only thing they could do was to pray. Melissa broke the deep silence. She turned to Judith with a sorrowful enquiry: "Do you understand what Dad was trying to tell me?"

Judith rubbed her face with her hands, trying to soothe her puffy eyes. She let out a deep sigh. "No, unfortunately I have no idea."

Crushed with defeat, Melissa's shoulders sunk. Her gaze was dull, but her words were full of hope as if they were affirmations for everything she yearned for. "Anyway, he'll talk about it all at length when he gets better."

That night, without having the chance to say anything further, Bard passed away, taking all his secrets with him to his grave. In his last breath his eyes opened slightly, a single teardrop rolled down his lashes and then his gaze froze. His beloved wife and only daughter were holding his hand as he made his way to eternity.

The moment she realised that he was gone, a scorching flame set ablaze in Melissa's heart and devoured her whole being. She was burning alive. It was such a fire that oceans would not be able to put out. Sobbing, she embraced her father and kissed him for the last time…

When Judith held her husband's face in her shaking hands, she took one good look at him; she scanned every detail as if to burn his image to her memory. Her whole body was trembling.

"Goodbye, my love, my sweetheart." Then emptiness…

A life with all its joys and sorrows, gains and losses; all that was known of him and all that was unknown; a whole life was sublimed into a teardrop and softly slipped away.

Chapter 4

Scotland, 1969

THE RAIN, WHICH HAD BEEN POURING INCESSANTLY FOR days, finally subsided. A heavy mist had fallen instead and enveloped the earth around them, enshrouding everything like the sadness that took over Bard's heart. He was not able to see what lay ahead, yet he went on guided by intuition. He was not sure whether he was moving ahead or moving in circles. He stirred awake early in the morning, forced himself to stay in bed and sleep for a little while more, yet he gave up eventually and decided to respond to the mystical call of the day's dawn. He wore his boots and stepped out. The air he inhaled in deep breaths was scented with moss, tree wood and sea salt. Despite the cool calming air, the heaviness of his spirit prevented him from finding relief. He climbed up the hills, accompanied by the gentle splash of the creek, which flowed a long winding path before it reached the sea. He hoped in vain that the mist would dissipate as he walked, and his vision would clear. The grief he felt expanded beyond his own self and ensnared the whole city. When he reached the hill where the trees got scarce and the fields extended, he sat down on a large rock, his usual place, hugged his knees to his chest and looked vacantly to the horizon. As time passed the fog dissipated; the landscape with the green countryside meeting the grey sea and the houses arranged in a colourful order were now visible. It was as if a cloudy curtain was raised, revealing a window opened to perpetuity. This was what he used to liken this sight to, a window to perpetuity… Yet now it looked like an abyss. There was nothing there… How much he used to love this place once.

This place and these melodies… Now all he could think about was to run away as far as possible. If he stayed, he would never be able to get rid of these dark clouds hanging over his head; it was only going to get worse.

When the rain started to fall, Bard pulled away from his thoughts, tilted his head to the sky and as he felt the rain trickling on his face and sliding down his cheeks, he thought, *I wish the rain could wash away all these thoughts in my head.* He got up and stared at the landscape, trying to engrave it into his memory. His tears were mixing in with the rain on his face. He knew that this was the last time that he was seeing this.

When he returned home, his father Richard was awake, preparing breakfast. He observed his son worriedly. "Good morning! What were you doing outside in this pouring rain? You are drenched."

Bard spoke with a cynical smirk as he hung his navy-blue raincoat, dripping with water, on the hanger by the door and took off his boots. "As if there are any mornings here without the pouring rain…" He took a towel from the bathroom, and as he dried his wavy ginger hair, he walked to the kitchen. While Richard cracked some eggs on the stove, he sliced the bread and set a fork and knife on the table. Their kitchen was tiny, with hardly enough space for the two of them to fit together, even without all the clutter…

They sat around the table in the living room and ate their meal in silence. When they were finished, Bard regarded the room where he had been born and raised. His eyes caught a photograph taken with his mother. They looked so much alike: the same hair, the same slender face. He sighed longingly as he thought, *I wish she was here with me.* He shifted uncomfortably in his chair, then suddenly uttered what was on his mind: "I can't stay here any longer, I want to go to America."

For a while, Richard studied the coffee cup before him in order to hide the disappointment in his eyes. Only when he thought he was able to control the motion in his gaze did he direct it to his son. He felt the blood in his veins freeze with the thought of losing his son, after the loss of his wife. He spoke, trying to keep his voice from shaking. "I do understand how you feel, son. That was all I wanted to do when

I lost your mother as well – one might say that I also ran away, by spending all my days and nights in that pub. All my friends, everyone I knew there would tell me that I'd drank enough, that I should go back home to you; they would order me food so I would not get dead drunk. I would get furious at their meddling and drive them away. But I have to tell you, son, running away is never the solution. Wherever you go, the pain follows."

Whenever he looked back on those days, Richard was overcome by shame and regret. Although he was not yet even sixty, he looked in his seventies with greying hair, sunken shoulders and deep wrinkles on his face. In the last two years he had aged almost ten years. As he was lost in thought he was shaken aware by Bard's voice. "You may be right, but that's the only way out I can think of right now."

Richard did not think his son's decision was right. Still, he could not bear to see him so unhappy and desperate. If he were to hold him back now, he was not only worried that Bard might blame him in the future but also that he himself may regret not letting him go. Maybe he should give this a chance. "But how are you going to survive there? What do you plan to do, music?"

Bard's gaze was tired, timid and even a little hateful. "Never! Music has no place in my life anymore. I will do anything but that."

With every inch of his soul, Richard felt the grief of knowing that his son would not come once he was to leave this place. *Life is testing me with the loss of my loved ones*, he thought, his shoulders sinking deeper. The acceptance of his demise was evident in the tone of his voice.

"Well, son, as far as I understand you have already made up your mind. Then I can offer you nothing but my support." He reached out to the hands of his son with a tender touch.

Bard's eyes glazed over; the lump in his throat made his voice come out with a slight quiver as he said, "Thank you."

As they cleared the breakfast table and tidied the kitchen together, Richard was still grappling with his worries and troubles, figuring out what to do. All of a sudden, he was stirred by an idea that came to his mind. "A good friend of mine immigrated to America years ago; after he settled down, he sent two or three cards with his address on them. I remember keeping those cards somewhere, I hope I recall correctly."

He had already started searching around as he spoke. Bard was also eager. He was happy that his father was not thoroughly heartbroken.

"Let me take care of the kitchen. You can look for the cards in the meantime."

Richard was giving his son some information as he kept searching through the possible whereabouts of the cards. "Malfoy was a steadfast friend; I have no doubt that he will do all he can to help. If you can get a hold of him, knowing you're with him would bring me some comfort as well."

He found what he was looking for as he was rummaging through the drawers of the dresser in his bedroom. He held the cards towards Bard and waved them in the air, smiling triumphantly. "My memory hasn't deceived me."

They spent the next few weeks preparing for his travels. Richard wrote a letter to Malfoy stating that he would be grateful if he could help and take care of his son Bard. He made two copies of the letters and mailed one of them while handing the other to Bard in case the mail didn't reach the addressee.

When the day of their separation dawned on them, Bard, his father and his close friend Sean stood on the ferry dock. The air was heavy, like his heart, and the sky was overcast with dark grey clouds. Unease surged in his stomach like the waves in the sea. Fear followed the feeling of excitement, which was then shadowed by a wave of sadness; the constant shift of his emotions overwhelmed him. His brown pupils looked larger on his blanched face. He felt as if he could give up if only someone insisted that he not go. But no, there was no turning back now, no matter how scared he was. He turned to his father with sadness in his eyes as the ferry he was about to get on approached the port with its long whistle blazing. "It pains me to leave you here alone, but I cannot stay here after what I have gone through. I have to go."

Richard's sleepless, tired eyes were glossy with tears. He put his bony hand on Bard's shoulder. "Don't think of me, son, I'll take care of myself. I'm not alone, I have my friends here – all I want is your happiness." He then placed his other hand on his shoulder and gently shook him. "Will you be fine there?"

Bard's lips were trembling; his eyes were red. "I'll try, Father."

"If it doesn't work out, know that you can always come back home. If there is any trouble, we will always be here waiting for you."

They hugged tightly. Richard placed his hand on Bard's neck and smacked his back, trying to enliven him. Both were no longer able to hold back tears.

"I love you, son. Don't keep me unaware."

Bard sniffed as he dried his cheeks with the back of his hand. "I love you too. Take care of yourself, mind your health and try not to worry about me, will you?"

Richard forced a smile. "I think I'm getting old; look at me all sentimental and soppy."

When it was time to say goodbye to Sean, Bard paused for a few seconds and looked into his friend's eyes, trying to find the right words. "Your friendship meant a lot to me. I don't know what I would have done without you, I'm thankful for you."

Sean pursed his lips and shrugged. "Nothing to be thankful for. What is friendship if it's not being there for each other through the tough times?" He softly thumped Bard's arm with his fist. "This place won't be the same without you. Who else am I going to jam with?"

Dark shadows passed over Bard's gaze for a brief second. "You know that it is over for me Sean. You are a good musician; you'll do just fine by yourself."

Frustrated by his own thoughtlessness, Sean changed the subject. "Don't worry about Richard, I'll take care of him. You just try to go build a good life for yourself there."

They hugged as they shook hands. When the ferry's whistle was blown once again, they all stared at the direction of the sound for a moment.

Sean turned to his friend and smiled proudly. "You are a brave man and I know you can do whatever you set out to. Go forth and conquer."

As the ferry moved slowly, the land got smaller in Bard's vision whereas his fears grew. Still, no fear could be greater than the remorse he felt. *Goodbye, sounds; goodbye, melodies,* he mulled. The thought brought him some solace. A brand-new life and a completely different world awaited him. There would be no more whispers; he had left them all in Scotland. He was now heading towards a new horizon.

The thought of finally being unshackled from his burdens calmed and comforted him.

How strange life was... This time last year he was thinking, dreaming of such different things, but now...

Chapter 5

United States, 2016

After leaving Ron, Melissa moved in with her mother Judith. Her mother's care and affection helped her greatly, not long after the breakup; in about two months she overcame her state of anguish.

Every evening, the mother and daughter sat on the chairs near the fireplace and chatted, like they used to do with Bard. They reminisced about him. Doing something for her daughter was also good for Judith, as it kept her busy and vibrant. They often visited Bard's grave and brought him flowers.

Melissa was working hard in the clinic, as usual. Whenever she got caught up in her work, she forgot about the troubles of her past and the worries of her future. At those times, she was truly in the moment. For now, her only plan for the future was to accept the guidance of her father's words and travel to Scotland. Her co-worker was on annual leave, so as soon as she got back, Melissa was going to take some leave and wend her way.

⌒

Melissa was standing in her room in front of the closet, playing pensively with her hair and trying to choose clothes to pack to her suitcase.

Judith knocked on the door and peeked in. "Do you need help?"

Melissa smiled with her hands on her hips. "Oh, I'd love it if you could help me, actually. I just can't decide. I do not want to carry too much; but I also don't want to take anything out in case I might need them."

Pushing aside the open suitcase on the bed, Judith sat down and ran her eye over the mess of clothes inside her daughter's closet with a smile. She never was able to imbue her daughter with a sense of orderliness no matter how hard she tried. Whenever she warned her, she received the reply, "Why should I waste time organising when I can easily find everything I'm looking for as it is?"

She stood up, picked a white and a green sweater from the pile and handed them to Melissa. "These look great on you; they bring out your lovely ginger hair and your green eyes."

Melissa folded and placed the sweaters in the suitcase. Her hands lingered on the white sweater; her mind drifted to two years ago, to that Christmas when her father was still alive. She smiled wistfully. Judith understood what she was thinking of; she looked at her with a forlorn gaze.

"Your father went Christmas shopping alone since I was too ill to join him. When he brought this sweater over, he said, 'As soon as I saw this, I could envision how beautiful Melissa would look in it.' He had good taste."

Melissa reached out and took her hand. "He sure did. After all, he chose you."

~

When the departure day arrived, Melissa was unable to contain herself. To know that she was going to be able to fulfil Bard's wishes, to finally learn about his past, thrilled her to no end. Strangely enough, she also felt as if she was going to Scotland to visit her father, as if she was going to meet him there. Melissa gazed at her childhood home one last time before she and Judith left for the airport. As she closed the door, her mind was busy with the question, *Will I be the same when I get back?* Her father's voice rang in her ears, whispering, "Fairy, music, cave, burden."

Judith called out to her anxiously. "Come on, hurry up! We are running late."

There was a lot of traffic, so the cars moved slowly. Judith was complaining about the congestion, but Melissa was aware that she had a lot more on her mind.

"I wish you would come with me, Mother; I don't feel at ease leaving you here."

Keeping her eyes on the road, Judith reached out and caressed her hand. "It is a long flight, darling – besides, I'm not sure if I want to learn about your father's past. I don't think I can muster that strength in me. You should go and get all the answers you need. For now, I'm happy with what I know. Maybe in the future…"

They almost crashed when the vehicle in front of them braked suddenly, coming to a screeching halt. When the driver got out and ran in front of his car, Melissa also got out and walked towards the same direction. A dog was lying on the ground, whimpering. The man looked terrified as Melissa looked at him enquiringly.

"It suddenly jumped in front of me."

The man let out a sigh of relief as he heard Melissa say, "I am a veterinarian."

"I hope there's nothing serious."

Melissa kneeled beside the animal and spoke in a calming tone as she scanned its entire body with her hands like an X-ray machine. A small crowd gathered around them, curiously watching. As the dog's whimpers slowly faded, the fear in its expression gradually gave way to curiosity; soon it began to show affection by wagging its tail. The dog stood back up as soon as Melissa pulled her hands away and rushed away as if nothing had happened.

With the peace of mind at knowing she could help, Melissa shouted, "Be careful from now on!" Then she turned to face the driver and reassured him: "I believe he was just very scared."

The man was surprised as he thanked Melissa; he was sure that he had hit the dog and hurt it badly.

Judith looked hopeless when Melissa got back in the car. "It would be a miracle if we can make it."

"I'm sorry, Mother. I just couldn't ignore that accident. I had to help." With a sparkle in her eyes and an easy conscience reflecting on her bright face, she added triumphantly, "Besides, I believe in miracles."

Chapter 6

United States, 1969

WHEN BARD ARRIVED IN AMERICA, HE HEADED STRAIGHT to the Baltimore address that his father had given him. He was overcome by an intense feeling of loneliness and fear. It was as if a deep void was surrounding him. What if he couldn't find anyone? What if he was truly all alone in this city? The worry was gnawing at him. His heart pounded in his ears when he reached the street where the house was located.

It was a spacious, wide street. Most of the buildings were two-storey houses with green lawns and parking lots in front and flowers hanging on their porches. The neighbourhood had a peaceful and quiet vibe; it seemed like it was mainly inhabited by families.

When he arrived at the brick building and saw the red door, Bard knew he was in the right place. The vines climbing the walls and the roses in the garden evoked a Scottish flair. It was almost noon, so there might not be anyone in. When he rang the bell and started waiting, he felt like time stood still.

Fortunately, a small, chubby, smiling woman in her late sixties opened the door before long. She had an apron on and was drying her hands on a small towel. "How can I help you, child?"

Bard was reassured, as he noticed her slight Scottish accent. "I'm looking for Malfoy Smith, ma'am."

"Wait a bit while I go get him, will you?"

Bard sighed with relief. When the door opened again, Malfoy

Smith was standing in front of him. He was a medium-height man with a slight paunch and greying ginger hair.

"Yeah, lad, why do you ask for me?"

Bard introduced himself and passed him his father's letter. Just as they expected, the letter had not yet reached him by mail yet. They invited Bard in.

Just like the exterior, the inside of the house was reminiscent of Scotland as well. The fireplace in the middle of the living room wall divided the space with a comfortable sofa and a television in front of it on one side and two wing chairs facing each other on the other side. Bard's grew pale upon noticing the bagpipes in the corner. Was he going to fall back into all those things that he'd crossed an ocean to get away from? After they sat down on the opposite wing chairs, Malfoy started to read the letter, while Bard turned to Mrs Smith and, pointing to the bagpipes, he asked with a feigned smile, "Does Mr Smith play the instrument?"

Enya's chubby cheeks blushed as she smiled; she waved her hands in the air with a mischievous glow in her eyes and giggled.

"Malfoy and music belong to two different worlds. I think this is the first time that I'm hearing those two words in the same sentence."

Inadvertently, Bard let out a faint laugh upon hearing her answer. Enya's heartfelt and genuine attitude was contagious and quite comforting.

Having finished reading the letter, Malfoy folded it up and put it on top of the fireplace, with a warm smile on his face. "So you really are our Richard's wean. It has been so long since I last heard of him, I thought he forgot me." He leaned forward and touched Bard's knee lightly. "Your father must have told you; he was a good friend of mine. We grew up together. Those were good days," he said with his wistful eyes looking vacantly into distance. "We didn't have much but we were happy." He placed his arms on the armrests comfortably. "You are a son of mine as well – consider this your home." He then turned to his wife. "Right, Enya?"

"Sure, you can stay as much as you want, dear."

Enya's motherly, soft appearance stirred one to squeeze her cheeks and give her a kiss. She got up and extended her hand to Bard. "Come on, let me show you the room you will stay in; you have come a long way, I'm sure you are tired." She grabbed Bard by the arm and guided him.

Bard took his suitcase and followed her upstairs.

Enya opened the door to a room. "This was our son's room; he now lives in San Francisco." She held the door open to let Bard in. "Rest well, you are welcome to join us downstairs whenever you want."

Bard gave her a grateful look. "Thank you."

When he was alone in the room, he flopped on the bed and spread his arms widely as if to embrace his new room and new life. After a long journey, he had finally reached his destination. With the peaceful serenity of having found safety, he closed his eyes and fell into a deep sleep.

It was dark when he woke up; when he turned on the bedside lamp on the nightstand to check the time, he saw a photo of a smiling man looking back at him. *This must be their son, he looks so much like his mother*, he mused. He got up as he realised that he must have been sleeping for quite a while. He scanned the room as he walked around. He approached the window with brown curtains and looked out. Just in front of him, there was a large plane tree painted by the light from the streetlamp. The sight of it struck a chord in his heart. He reminisced about a day from his childhood when he and Sean had climbed a plane tree in the park. Bard could not go down; they had to call for his father. He wiped his tears with his hand and sniffed silently. He took a deep breath; he had to pull himself together. He checked his watch again: it was seven. He quickly changed into a fresh set of clothes. When he opened the door, the sweet smell rising from the kitchen downstairs made his empty stomach rumble.

The table was already set and they seemed to be waiting for him. They all sat down to eat as soon as Bard came in. The steak and potatoes were delicious; Bard had started eating with a huge appetite but was full before he could finish half of his plate. He seemed to not be able to stomach much; it was also vexing for him that the main topic of conversation around the table was Scotland. Of course, his hosts wanted to ask him about Tobermory and its residents. Bard tried to fulfil their curiosity, answering their questions with a tingle in his heart and a knot in his throat. These good people had welcomed him to their homes; he could not be so ungrateful to only think of himself at a time like this.

When the conversation died down at the end of the night, he returned to his room and realised that the talking was just as tiring as the journey. He felt drained. The moment he lay down on the bed, he fell asleep, slipping into senseless dreams.

It was almost noon when he got up and went downstairs the next day. He heard the quiet rattle coming from the kitchen and headed there. He called to Enya, who was working facing away from him.

"Good morning."

Enya turned and smiled tenderly. "Good morning, child, did you sleep well?"

"Oh, I slept like a log…"

Enya gestured at the table and ordered him like a protective mother: "Sit down now and eat well for breakfast – you didn't eat much in the evening. I'll make some eggs and bacon; would you like that?"

"I'd love it."

Bard ate hungrily this time. Enya, sitting opposite him, reminisced about the conversations she used to have with her son and realised that she missed the feeling.

She didn't want to pry, but she couldn't help but ask as they sipped on their coffees. "What made you fly all the way across the pond to here?"

Bard had expected this question; his answer was ready. "Tobermory is a very small town, I couldn't see a future for myself there."

Enya raised an eyebrow in slight disapproval. "That's all well, but how did your father agree with you being alone here at such a young age? I wouldn't dare."

Bard straightened up; he was not going to allow anyone to criticise his father. "He was worried as well, but I had already made my decision, so he was left with no choice. I'm eighteen years old, after all."

Enya quickly realised that this was a sensitive subject. She backtracked, worried that she might have hurt his feelings, and feigned an angry tone as she spoke with a smile: "Oh, you youngsters do whatever you set your mind to."

Bard really liked the Smiths; they were very welcoming and it was a joy to live with them. However, he wanted to stand on his own two feet; he had to forget everything and start his new life as soon as possible. All their conversations revolved around Scotland, which didn't make it easier for Bard. He had to find a job and start earning money as soon as possible. The newspaper ads were a good start. He would scan the vacancies every day, noting the ones he thought that he might be qualified for and attending interviews. Other times, he would visit cafes, restaurants and markets to ask whether they were looking for any help. After two months with no progress, Bard was getting desperate and frustrated when he finally came across a 'Help Wanted' sign on the window of a small family-run restaurant named 'M&J' and went in.

The place was clean and neat; it had a reassuring atmosphere. The owners seemed nice as well. In the duskiness of the restaurant, a single table was lit by the fresh light of the morning; there the owners, the Crown couple, were sitting. As Bard made his way towards the wooden bank with the green leather cushions, he felt like a dragonfly trying to find its way by flying to the light. This place enveloped one with a sense of serenity. The only thing that troubled him was the music playing. He wished it could be a quiet place, free of music and melodies, but he knew that was out of the question. Bard explained that he had just moved here by himself from Scotland, where he used to work as a waiter, and that he was staying with the Smiths, who were helping him settle. Mary and John Crown were a friendly older couple. Bard's trusting appearance made them feel protective over the young man, while his courage impressed the couple; thus, they gave him a job.

Bard was going to stay in the attic room above the restaurant; he was also going to get a small salary. He felt good about these developments. He now had the two things he wished for: a job and a place of his own. His good luck had provided him with a glimmer of hope for his future.

After the dinner at the Smiths' house, Bard had insisted on clearing the table and tidying up the kitchen. When he was done, he moved into the living room, placed a chair in front of the old couple and sat down to give them the news.

Malfoy urged him with a slight grin. "Well, go on, tell us."

When Bard told them of his new job, they were happy for him, albeit a bit dejected that he was leaving. Their monotonous life had been livened up and refreshed by his arrival; it felt just like before, when their son still lived with them.

Enya forced a smile. "You could continue to stay with us here."

She turned and looked at her husband, her eyes asking for his support. Malfoy got up and poured a glass of whiskey. He knew that his wife was trying to make up for the absence of their son with Bard's company; in fact, this was true for him as well. As he sat back down in his armchair, he took a sip of the drink.

"Enya is right. You could just commute to work from here. We consider you a son – this is your home."

Although Bard didn't want to upset these good people, he had to go his own way. He glanced gratefully at the couple. "Thank you very much, I can't even imagine what I would have done without you. But I am going to be working late nights, it would be difficult to commute back and forth from here. Since I already have the option of staying there, I think I should just take it."

Enya drew near and put her hands on his cheeks. "Just promise to drop by often, okay?"

"Of course, you are the only family I have here."

Enya was almost going to break out in tears; she kissed Bard's cheeks and left the room in a rush like she was running away.

Bard hung his head. "I think I upset her."

Malfoy reached out and squeezed his shoulder. "No, she just got accustomed to your presence. Not just her – both of us got used to having you around. You are doing the right thing by leaving."

Mary Crown had cleaned and ventilated the room and put clean sheets on the bed. Although it was a small space, it had everything he could need. The pale blue wallpaper gave a calm feel to the room while the wood ceiling provided warmth. The window opening to the sky above the wrought-iron bed was going to bear witness to many of his sleepless nights, on which Bard would lie awake and look out into the stars. As Bard marvelled at his new room, Mary opened the other door of the room just next to the entrance door.

"This is the bathroom, there are some clean towels hanging behind the door."

Bard nodded.

Mary closed the door and showed him the closet at the foot of the bed. "You can put your stuff in here."

The gratitude and astonishment reflected in Bard's voice as he spoke: "Thank you, this place is amazing. Frankly I was not expecting to have such comforts."

Although her silver hair, her ice-blue eyes and the plain brown dress buttoned tightly around her neck gave Mary a stern and cold appearance, when she glanced at Bard, the icy waters of her eyes were warm like turquoise of the tropical seas; she smiled warmly. "I'm glad you like it. You can come join us downstairs after you're settled."

Just when she was making her way to the door, she turned and extended her hand. "I almost forgot; this is the key to the room."

After Mary left, Bard sat down on the bed and glanced around. Strange emotions flooded through him in waves. His heart was split in two. Half of it was pitch black, filled to the brims with sorrow. On the other half, thanks to all the lovely people he had met since his arrival here, there were sprouts of hope blossoming and the blackness was slowly being aside with first lights of the dawning horizon. Although he missed his father, his old home, he knew that this would never have happened if he stayed.

The rather small restaurant was charming with its red and white chequered tablecloths. When Bard walked in, Mary and John were sitting at the same glass table from yesterday, drinking coffee. John gestured towards the pot. "You can get some coffee for yourself, son. Come and sit down."

He timidly perched on the edge of the bench opposite them. They told him everything he needed to know about the functioning, the order and the rules of the restaurant, and explained what they expected from him.

Bard was confident that he could meet these expectations without difficulty. He had experience from his time in the O'Canon restaurant. One of the reasons he liked this place was that it resembled his old place of work. The waves of longing crashed on the shores of his soul as he reminisced; he wished Sean was here with him.

But now, he had to focus all his attention on his work in order to not disappoint these good people who'd given him a chance.

Bard learned all the details in no time and started to sail through his duties in the restaurant. He did not dawdle for even a second; he constantly found something to busy himself with, so he would not have to be alone with his thoughts. The more tired he was in the evenings, the sooner he could get to sleep without thoughts rushing into his mind. The melodies had been silent ever since he'd arrived in this country and the quietness of his mind was thoroughly soothing.

He got up early in the mornings, readied the restaurant for the day, made coffee and waited for Mary and John. Unlike Mary, John had a rather witty and easy-going manner. Though the restaurant had a cook, John enjoyed helping out and spending time in the kitchen. He loved eating as much as he loved cooking. That much was not difficult to make out from his chubby stature. Mary and him often bickered playfully about the issue. Mary was a meticulous woman who paid strict attention to eating well and healthily, to always be clean and neatly dressed. As a matter of fact, the couple complemented each other. Bard's duties at the restaurant was to prepare a list of groceries and necessities, go shopping, and to mind the register when the customers were around. He would help with the customers' orders, service and cleaning. After work, he would go up to his room, throw himself on the bed and drop off to sleep. As he had his meals at the restaurant and he didn't have many other expenses, he could save most of his salary. He sent half of his first salary to his father along with a letter. He wrote at length about his new job, the kindness of the Crowns and his comfortable life in the new country. He assured his father that he had nothing to worry about since he had no troubles other than missing him.

When he was not working Bard did not speak much; he usually gave short, simple answers when he was questioned about his life. He was a mystery to those around him. No matter how hard they tried, the Crowns could not find out anything of significance about his life in Scotland, his family and why he was alone in this foreign country. The only thing they knew was that his mother had died when he was sixteen and his father was still alive in Scotland. As time passed, they learned to take him as they found him. He was a good, decent and hardworking young man, and that was all that mattered.

＊

Years passed; Bard was now utterly competent and ardent in running the business. As Mary and John grew older, they started visiting the restaurant less and less frequently. Bard had been their right-hand man not only at work but throughout their personal lives as well. He tried to take care of the old couple just as they had taken care of him when he was still a young man. He wanted to do the same for his father, Richard, as well. He insisted that Richard come and live with him, but he could only persuade him to visit. When Richard came to see him, he could only stay for a month. He went back to Scotland, claiming, "It gets harder to get used to new environments after a certain age. Back home I have a life to which I am accustomed, don't make me give up that comfort." While some seniors wished to set sail for new adventures in the final years of their lives, others, like his father, were content staying in their safe haven.

Bard was just making a list of necessities when he looked up and saw Mary and John walking through the door. John spoke cheerfully. "Do you have any coffee for us, son?"

They walked towards the seats by the window, where they always sat.

Bard was puzzled as he took Mary's hand and helped her sit down. He raised his eyebrows. "To what do I owe the chance to see you so early in the morning? Everything's alright, I hope."

Mary stroked Bard's hand on her arm; the lines around her eyes deepened as she smiled. "No, no, dear. Come on, pour us some coffee, we just came to have a chat."

Bard bowed his head slightly, still confused. "A chat so early in the morning, huh!"

He went to the kitchen and came back with three cups of coffee and fresh chocolate-chip cookies. He looked at the two of them with worry in his gaze. "So how are you two, are you in good health?"

"We are fine, everything is fine, we are very happy," Mary said, then she turned and winked at her husband.

Bard was at a loss; they were acting strange. "Great, I hope you are always happy."

John took a sip of his coffee. "Aren't you going to ask for the reason for our happiness?"

Bard approached them as he put his elbows on the table and placed his head in his hands, then, with curiosity, he asked, "Is there a special reason as to why you are so happy?"

The husband and wife held hands, exchanging smiles and loving glances. John motioned for Mary, urging her to be the first to talk.

"We are going on a trip. We had been planning and postponing for years now, it's time to bring our plans to life. Long story short, we are retiring. We're thinking of finding a partner for our business here and handing the operations over to him, what do you say?"

A cloud of confused thoughts shadowed Bard's expression. His jaw tightened as he struggled to hide the disappointment in his eyes. There was a knot in his throat. "What can I say? I'm happy for you."

He had grown very fond of this place; he never thought he would have to face such a drastic change. His shoulders dropped and he grew pale. He tried to force an awkward smile. "Are there any candidates you are considering or interviewing?"

He was wishing that the new owner would be someone whom he could get along with when he heard John's fatherly booming in his ears: "We are considering you."

Bard was shaken up yet again. His eyes were out on stalks; his tongue was tied; he forced out a stammer: "I… I don't get it, how? I don't know if I have the finances to afford being a partner to this business."

John nudged his cup away from him and put his hands together on the empty space. "You are investing your labour and your time into this partnership."

Bard's confusion remained. With a dazed look he was trying to take in and comprehend all that he was hearing. "But that's not fair. I would never be able to pay for your support, both materially and spiritually, not even if I worked my entire life."

Mary took Bard's hand in her palms and caressed it; with a tender gaze she said, "You became our son and kept us company through all these years. Like any parent, we want to ultimately back away and give room for our children to be free."

A tear rolled down from Mary's bright blue eyes to her cheek.

Bard's eyes were also glazed over with the overwhelming love and gratitude he had. *What did I do to deserve such lovely people in my life?* he thought. His voice was trembling as he spoke. "I also consider you as family. I don't know where and how I would be now, if you were not here for me." He took a deep breath and continued. "So, let's make a deal; you'll have my labour and my time, as well as all of my current savings."

Mary was just opening her mouth to say, "We don't want your money."

However, Bard interjected with a determined voice: "I won't have it any other way."

John squinted; the creases around his eyes were more visible now. His soft cheeks drooped down as he was forced to accept what he was offered. He sighed. "Well, I know you, son, you're stubborn as a mule!" Then he shrugged and held out his hand to him: "All right then, partner." He turned and winked at Mary. "We've got ourselves a hardy partner."

They all laughed. Bard's eyes were sparkling merrily; he hadn't been this happy for as long as he could remember.

Bard was so caught up in work that he barely had any social life. Of course, love was also a distant dream. He dated and hung out with some people from time to time, but none of them turned out to be anything meaningful. The subtle music of love had stopped playing a long time ago for him. He had buried his emotions so far down in his memories that he wouldn't be able to revisit them even if he wanted to. To fall in love, to form a connection was like navigating with the moonlight on a cloudy night in the middle of the sea. When the moon disappeared behind the clouds, it all sank into darkness; one could easily lose their way and find themselves on distant, unknown shores. He was no longer a naive eighteen-year-old boy; he was able to control his emotions. Until... Until Judith started working at the restaurant.

Judith was of medium height. Her auburn hair framed her graceful face, which further accentuated her large moss-green eyes. The familiarity of her face shook Bard to his core when they first met. Her eyes were a mixture of his mother's and Maidie's eyes. Her affectionate manner, genuine gestures and deep, knowing gaze added substance to her simple beauty. She was quiet, sensitive and polite. She was hardworking, honest and responsible. All these features and all the similarities had inevitably made an impression on Bard. Even though he thought that it had been a long time since he had buried his emotions along with the memory of Maidie, over time he started to sense their resurgence.

Sometimes after finishing up with work and putting up the shutters in the restaurant, they'd share an evening snack, chatting for hours on end.

Talking to Judith was easy: she was a good listener; she was able to understand and empathise with people. She didn't overwhelm him with questions. She was able to remain sanguine even in the direst of situations. Sitting down and conversing with her brought comfort to Bard. The more he got to know her, the more he liked her and her company. It made him realise how lonely he had been.

Judith fell in love with Bard at first sight. His introverted silent, manner appealed to her. She could see that behind his serious, tough exterior he had a kind and caring personality. His behaviour towards the customers, the employees and the children was enough for her to understand that he did have a gentle soul. As she got closer to him, she started to gather that he had been hurt in the past and had developed this strong and stern outer shell in order to keep himself from ever getting hurt again. She was ready to do whatever she could to ease his mind and make him feel safe. It was not an easy thing to do, but she had the belief that she could overcome all difficulties through the power of her love; she knew that love's spark was an antidote to all that was evil, injurious and hostile. It was not hard to see why Bard was drawn to her, considering she had a kind heart full of love and compassion.

They got married a year after they had met, with a small, simple ceremony. Judith's family, the Smiths and the Crowns were invited to witness the young couple's special day. Bard longed for his father to come, but Richard's health did not allow him to set out on this long journey. "My heart is with you; I wish you all the happiness that the world can offer. I am also looking forward to meeting the bride. Don't keep me waiting for too long, come and visit me as soon as possible," he said.

Bard and Judith's daughter, Melissa, who was born after a year after their marriage, was the source of joy and happiness for both of them. With the birth of their daughter their lives gained a whole different meaning.

Chapter 7

Melissa, 2016

MELISSA WAS LYING DOWN ON THE UNUSUALLY comfortable seat of the plane, enjoying the drink she'd been served. This had been a complete adventure from the moment she had left the house. After the accident on the road, she'd arrived quite late at the airport; she thought she'd had missed her flight but fortunately it was delayed and she was able to get on the plane at the last minute. When she finally plumped herself on her seat, after that thrilling rush, she exhaled a deep sigh. After the take-off, she browsed through some magazines and newspapers for a while. She then found a good movie to watch, in order to get her mind off of all the uncertainties and questions. When the meal was served, she nibbled on it and drank some coffee. She finally drifted off to sleep while reading a book. In her dream, she saw her father as a young man, running towards her in a field with open arms. He smiled so tender and looked so gleeful that Melissa was still able to sense his warmth when she woke as if she was just cuddling him. When she fell asleep again after a while, she saw herself this time prancing in flowery meadows and flying above the clouds. With the pilot's announcement that the plane was starting to descend for landing, she slipped away from the clouds of her dreamland and started gazing into the clouds beyond the plane window. As the altitude lowered, London revealed itself in all its beauty. She was going to transfer from here. Melissa did not want to continue without rest after the long journey; she was going to stay in London overnight and then set off for Scotland the next day.

After passport control and baggage claim, she got into one of the classic black taxis of the city, waiting at the exit gates of the airport, and travelled to the hotel she was staying in for the night. The reception was in the entrance of this three-storey Victorian building near Hyde Park. She handed her credit card over to the clerk for payment, but the card was declined. Melissa was agitated by this slight issue taking place right at the beginning of her travels. She was already jet-lagged, was worn out emotionally, and all she wanted to do was to get to her room and have a good rest as soon as possible. Her shoulders collapsed in frustration and her face fell. She settled on paying in cash, then she made her way to her room.

She took a warm shower, then, wrapped in soft towels, she brewed some of the complimentary tea in the room, sat on the bed and put her feet up. Due to the time difference, she was not able to call the bank or her mother yet. She turned on the TV and zapped between the channels, then, unable to resist the heaviness of her eyes, she dozed off.

It took her a minute to shake off her confusion and realise where she was when she awoke. She stretched out her arms and arose, feeling rested. She took out her black sweatpants with purple stripes from her luggage, got dressed and put her hair up. She called her mother first, to let her know she was fine. She did not mention the little mishap with the credit card; there was no need to worry her. After her talk with the bank, she learned that her card was blocked from overseas use and it was going to take some time before she could do foreign transactions; the process to open it for international usage was going to take a while and since it was Friday it may only be done by Monday at the earliest.

Melissa didn't know what her situation would be in Tobermory; although she wanted to get there as soon as possible, she decided to wait here until her financial situation was certain, so she delayed her flight. She thought, *I'd better take a walk after ten hours of sitting on a plane seat*, then she put on her purple sneakers matching her sweatpants, took a tiny map from the lobby and went out.

Hyde Park was very close to her hotel, so she headed straight there. Luckily the weather was nice and even though the sun didn't warm her too much, its shine gave her some vigour. The trees and the leaves on the ground were painted in all the colours of autumn, creating a beautiful scenery. Upon seeing the sun, the Londoners took their children and their pets to have a sunny stroll outside. Some were sunbathing on the grass, some were running with headphones on, some were sitting on the benches and reading. The dogs were chasing after squirrels from one tree to the other while the squirrels were keeping an eye on passers-by to see if anyone would offer some food. Melissa felt sorry that she didn't bring any nuts to offer them. After a long walk, she settled on a bench in front of the Italian garden. She was looking around when she saw a father and daughter feeding birds a little ahead of her. Her heart dropped as she sat back, closed her eyes and reminisced about her father. As she thought of the times they spent together, she felt sorrow, joy, longing and love, all at the same time. The last time they were together when Bard was still alive and healthy, they were in a park. What she wouldn't give to be with him here now. "Thank you," she muttered, "for all the good memories." She wiped a single tear from her cheek.

⌒

She was studying the brochures she collected, while sipping her tea in the breakfast room of the hotel. She slept soundly last night and felt lively now. She thought, *Since I am already here, I might as well look around a little.* She made a list of places to see: Tower Bridge, Covent Garden, Trafalgar Square and Buckingham Palace. She took out a map and mixed in with the city crowd.

When she got back in the evening, she was very tired but glad. She literally fell in love with the city. It was the perfect harmony of old and new. Every nook and every cranny had the historical vibe of the past, but they also proposed the promise of the future. Just like Bard and Melissa...

It was rainy on Sunday, so Melissa decided to visit the museums. The first stop was, of course, the British Museum. It was noon when her quick tour around this magnificent museum was over. She visited Victoria & Albert and the Natural History museums for the rest of the day. When she returned to the hotel, her feet were aching, but she felt it was worth it. The more she explored this city, the closer she felt to her father. She sensed that her connection to her father's mysterious past was getting stronger as she got to know more of this country and the clouds of obscurity were clearing up. Considering how strongly she felt even in here, she could hardly imagine the effect that arriving at Tobermory may have on her.

At the end of the day, as she was sitting on a soft and spacious leather sofa in front of the window of a cafe watching the rain, she was startled by the realisation that her soul was at peace. 'Peace' was a feeling that she had long forgotten.

She was at the very beginning of her journey, but one thing she had already learned was that loneliness was not as difficult as she thought it would be. On the contrary, she liked being alone. She scheduled her day the way her heart desired and she changed her plans whenever she felt like it. She felt free like the birds roaming through the mountain peaks and endless valleys.

～

Melissa was going to arrive in Glasgow after a short journey of only one hour. Since the credit card situation had been resolved, she was now able to focus on her true objective. As the plane started to descend, lush green fields appeared through the clouds. As she watched curiously, dozens of questions meandered in her mind. What awaited her? Was she going to be able to find the answers to her questions? How was her life going to change once she got the answers she was looking for...? She knew that she was at a peculiar stage of her life; she felt deep down in her soul that her direction in life was completely changing. The interesting part was that it did not scare her at all. She was going to take a train to Oban from the airport right away. As she got closer to those places where her father grew up, her excitement grew; she did not want to loiter any longer. It was going to take a whole day for her to get to Tobermory. She bought coffee and croissants from the station for the three and a half-hour train ride, chose a table seat and sat down. It was an old train. The large windows let in the cold breeze of the outside and the frames rattled with the jolts of the wagon. Melissa felt like she was travelling through history. Like in that movie that she'd seen, she felt as if the train would soon pick up speed and return to the past, where she would meet her father as a young man. Who knows, maybe her father had gotten on this very train and sat down on the same seat. The thought of it warmed her soul.

She was gazing out from the window without a blink, admiring the view; she did not want to miss a single detail. The earth took on thousand shades of green; there were the magnificent warm colours of autumn spreading through the scenery as well. Yellows, reds and greens were almost competing to catch her eye. The train moved near a lake for most of her journey. A few houses were seen here and there with their backs against the forest, looking as if they were wallowing in the beautiful scenery unhurriedly. She felt the time moving slower around here, or maybe it had already stopped at some point in the past. The river running under the stone bridge, shrouded with a cloud of mist, seemed to have emerged from a fairy tale. The question of why her father left a place as beautiful as this and had never even gone back for a visit, was ever-prominent.

After she delighted her eyes on that beautiful scenery, Melissa's train finally arrived in Oban. The ferry to the Isle of Mull was leaving from right next to the station and the journey was connected. Thus, twenty minutes later, Melissa was sitting inside the all-glass passenger cabin of the ferry, hoping that the journey would not be too rocky. After some time, Melissa glanced back at the mainland the ferry was drifting away from, with a strange feeling in her soul. She felt that she had left all her burdens behind and was now floating freely in space. As she neared the end of the journey, she was plunging herself into her father's mysterious past, feeling slightly daunted but still strangely light and relieved.

When they arrived on the island after forty-five minutes, it was time to take the bus to Tobermory as the last leg of the journey. There were only five passengers in the bus and they all seemed to know one another. The driver seemed about Bard's age. Melissa's gaze softened as a thought crossed her mind: *Maybe he knows my father, maybe he is his childhood friend.* She was surveying the places they were passing through trying to etch the sights in her memory. The narrow roads were surrounded by pine forests and trees that were unknown to her. The areas where the trees were scarce were still blanketed with lush vegetation. They stopped by a small village and Melissa, who had yet to see any other settlement around, thought, *I wonder what it would be like to be young in a place like this, maybe my father found it desolate and boring.* She was scrutinising every detail in order to understand better. Eventually, after an hour, they reached Tobermory and Melissa got off the bus, waiting for a few seconds for the feverish tremble in her heart to subside. She closed her eyes and took a deep breath as she thought of her father. She could have sworn that she could smell her father's cologne in the gentle breeze from the sea. She smiled and whispered, "Here I am, Daddy; I came as you wish."

Overcome by emotion, with the hazy sight of Tobermory's colourful houses arranged in orderly lines, she thought that she had just stepped into a fairy tale. It was a magical, beautiful, warm tale... Was it going to have a happy ending? Melissa took another step forward with an intense longing in her heart and a burning ardour to solve Bard's mystery.

Chapter 8

MELISSA HAD BOOKED A HOTEL WITH A SEA VIEW. AS Tobermory was not a large town, it was not difficult to find the place she was looking for. This was a cosy, small family business with four guest rooms, with red-painted flowerpots in front of its entrance gates. The owners greeted her with a warm welcome and showed her to her room. It made Melissa feel like she was visiting an old relative's home.

She opened her suitcase and put her things in the closet and the drawers. She then went straight ahead to take a shower in the hope that it would help alleviate her fatigue after the lengthy journey. As the water flowed over her body, she felt that it washed away her weariness. Feeling refreshed, she wrapped herself in white towels, boiled some water using the kettle on the table opposite the bed and made some coffee. She sat down on the mustard-coloured velvet chair in front of the window and rested, gazing upon the sea view. Though she was away from her country, her mother, her friends and the world she was accustomed to, she did not feel lonely. She felt her father's presence inexplicably and she was at peace. The secrets that once frightened her did not affect her as much anymore. She was going to spend her time here not only trying to uncover the mystery of her father's past, but also to uncover her true self, her innermost feelings, desires and purpose in life. This journey was not only a gateway to her father's past but also to her present and her future. She had stepped off the threshold now and she had no chance of returning.

When her head fell forward, she was startled and realised she'd fallen asleep from exhaustion as she was sitting there.

Even though it was difficult, she forced herself to get up, put on her pyjamas and curl up under the soft quilt. In her dream, she saw her father with his arms open once again, saying, "Welcome." Even in her dream, she wished that the moment would never end. The day was about to break when she opened her eyes. She stretched on the bed and pushed the duvet away; when she got up and drew the velvet curtain open, the view she saw took her breath away. As the colours, which graded from pink to purple near the horizon where the sea and the sky met, captivated her soul; the rosy-red sun slowly rising seemed to be promising a beautiful day ahead.

After watching the sunrise, she put on her sweatpants and walking shoes, then went out. She had forgotten how much she loved this early morning sensation. Her busy life kept her from being mindful of all these things she adored. She made a mental note: *From now on, do more of what makes you happy and what you enjoy doing!* She smiled on her own and nodded, agreeing with her own decision. While walking along the beach, she inhaled deeply and filled her lungs with gulps of sea air. With the fresh scent of moss and sea, she sensed the existence of a completely different, beautiful life full of mysteries and surprises.

The grey sky and the blue sea were almost the same hue. It was not clear where the sea ended and the sky began. The greens, yellows and reds of the trees and the vibrant facades of the houses contrasted with this bluish-grey backdrop and added colour to the scenery. Melissa was enticed by the harmony of the colours.

Plane trees, acorns, oaks and many more looked as if they were dressed in carnival clothes. *I think that's why I love autumn the most,* Melissa thought.

She shuddered slightly, with a strange feeling. She felt as if she was gazing through her father's eyes just now and all the wonders that she discovered were delighting him as much as they delighted her. Forty-five years ago, her father was perhaps walking upon the same paths, looking out at the same view; who knew what he might have been dreaming of? Navigating her thoughts and emotions, she noticed that she had reached a park and was rather tired, so she sat down on the wooden bench under a great plane tree. There must have been a stream nearby, since she could hear the splashing of the water. She leaned back, opened her arms and looked up to the sky through the few leaves left on branches, trying to concentrate on the sounds of nature. Her father's laughter reached her ears. She remembered their walks in nature, watching the clouds and amusing themselves by likening the cloud shapes to various different things. When they met at the park that day, Bard had said, "I will tell you about Scotland and my past," yet he did not live long enough to share these things. Melissa sighed; she was so lost in thought that she did not immediately notice the panting noise near her. The realisation made her jump a little. The noise came from a pug with a black and off-white coloured coat. It was looking at Melissa with curiosity in its bright, bulbous eyes. She smiled and petted the dog.

"Hey, who are you, you sweet little thing? You scared me."

Meanwhile she heard a male voice calling out 'Foam'.

"So, you are called Foam, huh? Come on, run back. You wouldn't want your friend to be worried, would you?" But the dog did not move; its eyes were fixated on Melissa. Melissa picked it up. "Well then, let's go together."

She walked towards the direction of the voice. A man in his early thirties with an athletic figure and dark brown hair appeared from among the trees. When he extended his arms, the dog immediately leapt towards him.

"Oh, you spoiled girl!" he said, flustered. "I'm sorry, she doesn't usually run up to strangers like that; it's the first time this ever happened. I don't know why."

Melissa reached out with a smile to pet Foam's little head. "I don't mind it. I love animals, maybe she sensed that as well."

The young man held out his hand with a charming and friendly manner. "I'm William."

"Melissa."

"Are you here on a holiday?"

Melissa didn't feel like explaining the details of her trip to someone she had just met. "You can say that, I guess."

She petted the dog again, then, without letting the man ask any other questions, she said, "Nice to meet you both."

She turned around and followed the same path back to the hotel.

Melissa's stomach rumbled when she got a sniff of the delicious smell of freshly toasted bread. She had not eaten before falling asleep last night. She sat down at the table she was shown to then had a hearty breakfast of scrambled eggs, beans and strawberry jam. While sipping her tea from the elegant rose-patterned pink cup, she looked through the brochures that she'd taken from the hotel lobby. As expected, the brochures mostly consisted of tourist attractions. She thought that there must be a government office somewhere where she could look up documents regarding the population records or other information that could be useful for her search. She knew that hotel staff would probably help her if she were to ask, but this was a small town anyway and she wanted to explore, so she didn't think it would take her too long to find what she was looking for by herself.

Lucky for her, it wasn't raining, so she was able to travel around the town with no inconvenience. The few people she met were either locals or tourists who were on nature excursion tours. She was able to tell the tourists apart from the locals easily due to their clothes and their hefty backpacks. As far as she understood from the brochures, the town was frequented by those who enjoyed studying birds and marine animals. To witness the existence of such virgin lands for the animals to set up home in exalted Melissa. She toured the entire town, yet she did not come across a place where she could talk to an official, like a municipality or even a post office. She thought, *Maybe things operate differently in small towns like this. I'd better ask for someone's help when I get back to the hotel.* Then she headed for the hills, where there seemed to be no habitation. As she climbed up, the view waxed even more beautiful. After discovering the wilderness for about two hours, she returned to the town centre and entered the first restaurant she saw to grab a bite and rest.

The charming old restaurant she got in had a welcoming, warm feel to it. They showed her to a table by the window. When the waiter came with the menu, Melissa motioned with her hand dismissively.

"Never mind the menu, do you have anything you can recommend – a specialty, maybe?"

The waiter seemed glad to be able to provide an opinion; he

straightened his back and spoke confidently: "The baked fish with lemon sauce is our chef's favourite, I would recommend that for you."

"Okay, I'll have that and a glass of white wine."

Melissa studied the surroundings as the waiter walked away. The stone walls and wooden beams supporting the ceiling provided an authentic atmosphere. A large fireplace was burning in the middle of the hall; the crackling and sparking of the fire could be seen from every table. Melissa's eyes riveted on the stirring of the flames, and the beautiful scent of the burning wood, which pervaded the whole room, reminded her of those delightful conversations she had with her father on winter nights. With a longing sigh she pulled her eyes away from the fireplace and gazed out the window to see that it was raining. Raindrops were falling on the surface of the sea, piercing it with thousand holes then mixing in and becoming one with the vast body of water. As she stared at the landscape in awe, the carefully curated music for the restaurant reached her ears and enhanced the enchantment of her soul.

She ate her food with delight; the fish was delicious. The atmosphere, the scenery, the music, the food all appealed to her many distinct senses. Yet, it was time to focus once again on the matter at hand. She paid for her meal and got up. She was just making her way to the door when the photo frame hanging on the wall behind the cashier desk caught her attention. She approached with the waiter's permission. When she finally discerned the photo clearly, she could hardly believe her eyes. There were two boys in the photo, posing with their arms over each other's shoulders, one of which was her father. She was astonished to see her father's image so unexpectedly; she felt her heart beating in her throat. She gulped to overcome the choking sensation and, with a tremble in her voice, she asked, "Do you know who these boys are in the photo?"

The waiter pointed to the photo. "The one on the right is my boss Sean O'Canon, the owner of this place. I don't know the other one, but he must be someone important for Sean since his photo is hung right here."

Melissa asked, holding her breath, "And is Mr O'Canon here, can I talk to him?" She was hoping that the owner was still alive; the worry gnawed at her soul as she waited for an answer.

"He usually stops by here at about noon, you might get a hold of him if you come around tomorrow."

"Thank you, I'll definitely come tomorrow."

"Who should I say is looking for him?"

Melissa smiled. "He doesn't know me, but my name is Melissa."

She held back an excited scream when she finally walked out. She almost heard her father's laughter as she muttered, "Oh my, I am going to see someone who knows Dad from his youth." She looked around her but did not see anyone. She then gathered herself, shaking her head and thinking, *I am acting strange, the excitement got me in a flap.* She had to share the news with her mother as soon as possible.

She leapt straight to the phone when she entered her room. She was pacing up and down the room as she talked; she couldn't stay still. Only after she hurriedly broke the news to her mother was she was able to find some composure.

"It is as if Dad is here with me – I could swear I heard his voice earlier. I felt his support this whole time. What do you think of this, Mom? Do you think I feel him so close just because I wish it to be so or…? What should I believe?"

Judith tried to keep her voice from trembling; however, she was not able to conceal the longing in her tone. "Oh, my darling, you have such a delicate soul. Don't vex your mind with such worries. If this emotion heals and empowers you then so be it; stop trying to rationalise and just feel. I believe at this time of your life, you are going to need your intuition more than your mind. And whatever you may learn about your father, just keep in mind that he loved you very much and did all that he could to make us happy."

Melissa was sitting sideways in the chair with her feet dangling off the armrest; she was grinning placidly. "I'm telling you; you should have been a psychologist."

Judith smiled with a deep sigh. "I wanted to, but I couldn't at the time – maybe in another life… Anyway, it satisfies me enough to be of help to my loved ones. I love you, honey."

Melissa was fully settled. She took her book and lay down on the bed. After a while, just when she was drifting off to sleep, with the book dropping from her hands, her father appeared before her. "You have a special potential, discover it!"

His voice was so real that Melissa jumped from her sleep and checked around the room. She kept having these dreams whenever she fell asleep lately. She wasn't afraid, but it did feel bizarre. Was her mind playing tricks on her? *I'll do as my mother advised and won't question it*, she decided as she got up, got a glass of water and watched the world outside from the window as she sipped. She could not resist the tempting call of the beautiful scenery. It bothered her to sit around and wait anyway, so she wore her furry camel-coloured boots and a coat of the same colour, then rushed outside.

The coolness of the weather was quite refreshing. Passing the colourful houses on the beach, she followed the path that met the sea. There she leaned against the iron railing, stood and watched the day turn into night. When she arrived at the sign saying 'MYSTIC PUB' after a short walk with unhurried steps, the rain had already started to drizzle. The name of the pub compelled Melissa to go in and check out the place.

The venue was mostly furnished in dark blue and purple colours. The lights were dim, amplifying the striking unearthly atmosphere, which did justice to the name of the place. Melissa had read somewhere that purple did create such an ethereal impact. *So it's true*, she thought. The hazy light from the sconces and the sonorous Celtic music gave an authentic feel to the place. She was right to trust her instincts and go in here… The dark blue lacquered bar was shining with the reflection of spotlights on it. When she settled on the high stool, she turned to study the place once more from that point of view. Here in this pub, there seemed to be a world of contrasting binaries: the past and future, the dark and light, the mystery and clarity. The bartender, who was crouching down to get something out from the lower cupboards, stood up just when Melissa turned to face the bar, her head full of thoughts and observations. The two of them stared at each other in surprise. This was the owner of that dog that she'd encountered at the park yesterday morning. The first thing Melissa could think of was that this really was a small town. William was the first to speak. Dimples took shape on his cheeks as he smiled.

"Hello, Melissa, welcome to Mystic Pub."

Melissa responded with a reserved smile. "Hello, William, isn't it?"

William leaned towards her with his arms against the bar counter. "Yes. Yes, it is. How are you, how is your holiday going?"

Melissa thought that it would do no harm to be a bit more genuine, as she was impressed by William's natural, friendly demeanour. She tucked away the curl that fell on her cheek. "I'm fine, I am just slowly getting to know the surroundings," she said, shrugging, and she then continued with a smile. "Though I was done discovering almost everywhere in just two days, so maybe not so slow, right?"

William chuckled a little. "Well, welcome to our tiny town." He straightened up, still holding on to the edge of the bar. "What may I offer you?"

"Can I have some Irish whiskey, please?"

"Coming right up, miss."

William amicably winked at her and spun on his feet, then he reached towards a shelf, got the bottle and poured her drink with graceful motions. He added two ice cubes to the glass and placed it on the coaster. As he moved away to check on another guest, Melissa's curious green gaze followed him. When he turned abruptly as if he had felt her eyes on him, fire rushed to Melissa's cheeks. As William put down the utensils in his hand on the counter, surprised at her own keenness to converse with him, Melissa asked, "Have you been working here for long?"

The young man proudly looked around. "I guess you can say that I have, yes. I own the place."

"Ah! That's great." Melissa scanned the place afresh with admiring eyes. "Kudos to you, this place is beautiful and one of a kind. I really like it."

William nodded, straightening his shoulders and puffing out his chest. "Thank you, I'm glad you like it."

Melissa wanted to continue their conversation, but she was afraid that she might be distracting him. Looking around nervously, she saw that all customers seemed to be content for now; they all seemed to be in a good mood.

Sensing her concern, William smiled sympathetically as he

gestured at the customers. "They are our regulars; they just come and get whatever they want from the bar."

Melissa glanced in astonishment. How could he know what she was thinking? There was something extraordinary about this man. He was easy to speak to and easy to understand. She felt comfortable with him, as if she had known him for a long time.

"I love the decoration and the colour scheme. Did you get any professional help?"

"No, every detail is my own work. I think it is a way of self-expression, you know, how one styles the place where one lives. I think it is very personal; you can't call somebody else's creation yours."

The green of Melissa's eyes dulled; a cloud of gloom shrouded her gaze. Her heart sank as she recalled the house where she'd lived with Ron. Nothing about that place manifested Melissa's identity or presence. She only existed there in relation to Ron. She came back to her senses as she heard William's voice.

"So, what brought you to this island, to our small town?"

The gloom in Melissa's eyes made way to a pained gaze. "My father is from here – or he was from here. He passed away last year. I thought that if I were to visit the places where he was born and raised, I might miss him a little less."

"I'm sorry for your loss." Noticing the wave of emotions surging in the woman's eyes, William felt remorseful. Wishing to brighten her deep gaze, he dismissed the subject. "I upset you. Anyway, I'll change the subject. Do you like it here then? Was it up to your expectations?"

"Oh yes, it's a calm, peaceful place."

As William gave her a warm and sincere smile; his lovely dimples appeared once again. "It sure is calm."

When a customer called for him, he excused himself and left her side. When he was done attending the customer, Melissa had already finished her drink. She reached for her purse to pay.

William spoke determinedly with a stern look. "I do not take money from guests who have just come from far away to visit their father's homeland. This is my welcome gift for you."

Melissa thought of raising an argument but then decided it would be disrespectful to refuse the gift. She sighed. Her moss-green eyes glowed with a spark from deep within.

"Well then, I'll go now. Thank you very much both for the drink and your friendship."

When Melissa got back to the hotel, she fell asleep as soon as she lay on the bed, with the weariness from an exciting, busy day and, of course, with the warm tipsiness caused by the whiskey.

What woke her up with the first light of the morning was the same dream she had had every night since she started this journey. She was still under its influence when she opened her eyes. "Oh, Daddy!" she muttered to herself. She got up, rubbed her face and pulled herself together. She stood and stretched out at the edge of the bed; she then headed straight for the kettle like she did every morning. She made a cup of coffee and sat in front of the window with the cup in her hands. The gradient of colour, with red on the horizon, then pink and purple, heralded a new day filled with wholly new beginnings. A flock of seagulls flew hurriedly in the direction of the sun to witness the sunrise. Melissa could feel the flutter of their wings in her heart. For the first time her father's past was so within reach and that curtain of mist was soon going to be lifted. With the thoughts swarming through her mind, she was no longer able to stand doing nothing in the room. She wore a white turtleneck over her thermal tights, took her coat and stepped into the wintry air of this gorgeous morning, hoping to cool down the fiery fervour inside.

She felt the salty dampness of the cold breeze of sea descending to her lungs. It gave her some comfort. As always, greenery pulled her towards itself; she walked to the park in the distance. On her way, she saw a shop; she was surprised that it was open so early. She went in and got some peanuts. After walking on the paved path of the park for a while, she decided to stroll amongst the oak trees, shaking the bag in her hand trying to attract the squirrels' attention. She crouched down, put a few nuts on her palm and started waiting. After briefly hesitating, the bravest squirrel approached, then others followed and they all enjoyed the morning meal. Moments such as these were priceless to Melissa. She truly did love all animals dearly and felt at peace when she was with them. Right at that moment, Foam came running from afar, scaring away the poor squirrels, and settled in her arms with a sense of entitlement. Melissa responded to this show of affection with petting, caressing and cuddling the small dog playfully.

William drew closer to them; his eyes shone like sunlight. "Hey! Good morning."

Melissa's face shone with the same light as she looked up. "Good morning to you too. I see you are an early riser as well."

"I'm usually even earlier, I got up late this morning." He gestured to the squirrels. "I knew that you were quick to form a special bond with Foam, but I see now that you have a good relationship with all animals. I've been walking here for years; I haven't once seen these rascals come near people like that. You have something special."

Melissa glanced around with fondness. "I love them. Besides, I'm a veterinarian – it is my job to connect with them."

Without even noticing, the two started to stroll together. William didn't want to be nosy, but he was eager to get to know her. "Do you walk every morning?"

"I have since I arrived in Scotland, every morning and every afternoon. But I don't do it as often at home in America, unfortunately." She contemplated, *I should make a list of these things that I want to do more when I get back home.* She suddenly halted. She had a curious desire to share her excitement with William. "You know, I'm going to meet an old friend of my dad's today. He never told us about his life here, so this is very significant to me."

William was listening to her with his hands in his pockets; he looked at her with delight as he heard the thrill in her voice. "That's great, I'm really happy for you."

When they arrived at the exit gates of the park, William didn't want to leave. There was something different about this girl; she was unlike anyone he ever met. He was drawn to her in a peculiar way. As he asked, "How about continuing our conversation over a cup of coffee?", he wished dearly that she would say yes.

How could he have known that Melissa was befuddled by the very same emotions? William got the answer he wished for with the cheerful smile of the young woman.

"Alright, how can I say no to such a nice offer?"

When they entered the pub, Foam rushed to lie on a soft pillow behind the bar while William set out to prepare their coffee. Melissa's heart was drumming with all kinds of thrills as she settled in the navy-blue soft leather chair.

A short while later, William approached with steaming cups of coffee in his hands; he sat opposite her and leaned forward with his elbows on his legs, looking intently.

"You said you were going to meet with a friend of your dad's."

Melissa grabbed her cup with both hands and took a sip. "Yes, I will go see him around noon. I hope he can give me some information about my father's secretive past. As I said, his life here is a complete mystery to me. His mother died when he was little, and his father died when I was a baby. He was eighteen years old when he moved to America. That is all I know." Melissa's moss-green eyes sparkled with tears gathering at their edges.

William desperately wanted her beautiful gaze to sparkle with joy instead of melancholy. "I wonder who this person you are going to meet is? I probably know him."

"He is the owner of the restaurant where I ate yesterday. It was a coincidence actually; I was just leaving when I saw a photo of two young men on the wall and one of them was my dad. It was astonishing, really."

"Which restaurant is this?"

"O'Canon." Melissa raised her eyebrows when William burst out laughing. "What's so funny?"

"I didn't tell you my surname, did I?" He enjoyed the cute, surprised look that appeared on Melissa's face. "Sean O'Canon is my father." Knowing that he was finally going to be able to help her, William leaned backwards contently. "If I had known, I would have saved you from the anticipation and introduced you to him last night."

Her wide-open eyes blinking like two emerald stones, Melissa lifted her clasped fists over her agape mouth. Could all this be a coincidence? Her encounter with this striking, charming man, the friendship between their fathers, the ease with which she was able to reach what she was looking for... It was as if an invisible power was aiding her. Melissa felt in her heart that it was her father's doing.

"What a coincidence!"

An intense look of respect was visible in William's gaze. "So, the man that my father mentioned with great deal of regard for all these years, the man whom he called his brother, is your father."

The twinkling lights in Melissa's eyes hypnotised him with their sparkle. Her glowing red hair was falling in sparkling twirls over her light skin; William felt an irresistible pull towards her.

He shook off his emotions and got on the phone; when he was done with the phone call he turned back with his dimpled smile. "Are you ready? My dad is looking forward to meeting you."

Melissa felt like there were millions of balloons pulling her towards the sky, making her tread on air.

Sean was waiting for them when they arrived at the restaurant. After clasping Melissa tightly to his chest, Sean grabbed her shoulders and gently pulled away, studying her face with fondness.

"You look so much like him. Your ginger hair, your freckles, your stare... It is exactly the same. Come sit down, my dear girl, we have a lot to talk about."

With his shaking hands, he led Melissa to the table in the farthest corner.

Melissa felt like she was walking on a cloud; she was dizzy with excitement. Soon she was going to discover the enigmatic past of her father and maybe with this discovery she would also be able to understand herself a bit better as well. She sat down on the chair that Sean was pointing at, not knowing where to put her hands, and after a few anxious positions she decided to fold them on the table.

Sean's eyes were brimming with tears. Wholeheartedly hoping that there was a misunderstanding, he enquired, "William told me that he has passed away, is it true?"

"Unfortunately... He had a heart attack last year... It all happened so suddenly..."

A teardrop rolled down from Sean's cheek to his chin. "If I had known of you, I would have gotten in touch earlier."

Melissa couldn't understand why her father never mentioned such a loving friend who cared so much about him. "It is a complete mystery to us why he lived so detached from his past." Melissa hadn't noticed that she had torn a napkin in front of her into pieces as she spoke. She felt her mind was similarly torn.

Sean glanced at her with compassion as he reached out and patted her hand. "I'm sure it wasn't easy for him as well."

"He went in and out of consciousness while he was at the hospital – once when he was awake he told me to go to Tobermory. He muttered unintelligible words like 'talent', 'fairy', 'cave' and also the name 'Maidie'. My mother has no idea what these mean as well." She took a deep sigh and continued, "I think he wanted to share his secrets with us in his last moments, but there just wasn't enough time. I think he directed me here, so I can finally learn what he couldn't tell me." She glanced around and shrugged her shoulders with a bitter simper. "So here I am."

Sean took Melissa's hands in his palms, closed his eyes and envisioned Bard; the longing he felt for his friend ached in his heart. Yet, now he had to help this poor soul in front of him who, perhaps with slight remorse in her heart, questioned why her dear father never opened up his heart completely to her.

"Your father was a remarkable man. He was strong in his intuition and his emotions; he was also intelligent and hardworking. I'm guessing you are unaware of his musical genius."

Melissa gaped at him with astonishment; when she could finally find the words to say, she spoke stutteringly. "My dad and music? He wouldn't even let us listen to music, let alone make it."

For a brief minute an old memory flooded her mind and a vision slowly materialised before her eyes. She was about twelve or thirteen years old. She bought herself a music box with the pocket money she had saved. When the lid was lifted, a little fairy came out of the box dancing and turning with the music. Bard was mad with fury when she showed him her new toy; he took it away from her hands, hurled it across the room and broke it. Melissa did not understand what she had done to anger her dad so much; she cried herself to sleep.

Her mind foggy with memories, she was brought back to the present moment with Sean's voice as she was thinking, *What does it all mean?*

"I can understand your confusion. I will explain it all in detail, but first, we should go get your things and bring you home, then we can talk comfortably."

"Please don't trouble yourself, I have already settled in the Harmony Hotel."

Sean stood up; there was a fatherly feel in his determined expression. "That's very well, Harmony is a nice hotel, but I cannot let you stay in a hotel, like you have no friends or relatives in this town. Bard was my brother and you are a part of the family."

"Thank you very much. These words mean the world to me. I'd be happy to stay with you as well, I'm sure it would be much more comfortable than the hotel, but unfortunately I made the payment in advance." She looked at William, who was sitting quietly next to them, seeking his support.

The young man realised that she was trying not to hurt his father's feelings and interrupted, "She'll go to the hotel to sleep and spend the rest of her time at home with us. How does that sound?"

Melissa looked at him gratefully.

"Well, so be it," said Sean, pursing his lips.

William winked at Melissa secretly while Sean put Melissa's arm around his own, urging, "Now let's head home, we have a lot to talk about."

Sean and Cordelia's home was a typical British cottage-style house painted in white, with a dark-red wooden entrance door and colourful flowers in the hanging pots. Even with its exterior, the house warmed the onlooker's heart.

Cordelia greeted them with the same dimpled smile that her son often flashed. She sat Melissa down in a soft armchair patterned with flowers, opposite the burning fireplace in the living room, and glanced at her lovingly. "The tea is ready; I'm bringing some right away."

William was standing with his hands in his pockets, not knowing what to do, as Sean sat in the seat opposite Melissa. "I'll leave you two alone to talk comfortably."

Melissa was quick to interfere, astonished by her own desire to have his presence and support. "Please stay, you have the right to hear this story, after all you've done to help."

When William noticed the anxiety in Melissa's kind gaze, he muttered, "If you are sure then…"

71

Sean leaned back, placed his hands on the armrests, took a deep breath and spoke with a compassionate expression. "Yes, my dear girl, should I first explain those unintelligible words to you – cave, fairy and all that – or should I start telling you about it from the beginning?"

Melissa's heart started beating faster; her whole body tensed. "As you wish… I don't know a thing about his life here, so I'll appreciate it all the same. Since I don't know the slightest about his life here, whatever you say will be a new discovery for me."

Sean squeezed the bridge in between his eyes with his thumb and index finger and rubbed his eyebrows, as if he had a headache. "This story is not exactly a happy one – are you sure you want to hear it? I'd hate to see you upset."

Melissa shifted in her seat, straightened herself and nodded "Not knowing is the hardest. For better or worse, he is my father. Nothing I hear can change the fact that I love him. Learning about him could only make me understand him better. Please tell it all, I am listening to you with all my being."

Chapter 9

Bard and Sean were childhood friends. They grew up together; but what really tied the two of them together was their shared passion for music. They dreamed of starting a band and becoming famous one day. They both played the guitar well. Bard was also a good singer and a songwriter. His mother Angela was aware of her son's talent and she supported his endeavours to improve himself. She gifted him a high-quality guitar for his thirteenth birthday. Often, as Bard practised his guitar, she would leave what she was doing and listen to him intently, telling him, "You'll be a great musician someday," whenever she heard him play, with pride and hope in her sparkling eyes.

Bard spent his days going to school and studying music. He was a good student. His music teacher noticed his talent as well and informed him that he could get a scholarship at a good university if he kept his grades up and could even pursue a career in music, which kept him motivated in his studies.

It all was well for Bard. Until his mother's illness… Suddenly, their world turned upside down. For a while, his mother's complaints of mild back pain and coughing remained undiagnosed, with Angela not thinking too much about it as well. However, as the pain and coughing increased with the weight loss and weakness being added to her ailments, soon Angela realised that it might be something serious. By the time it was properly diagnosed the illness had already progressed beyond the point of recovery. It was lung cancer. The pain promptly became unbearable. The already petite woman grew ever thinner as her body fought with the illness; her beautiful beady eyes, which were always the most prominent feature of her face, grew even more noticeable and larger in her now-tiny face, her gaze deep and sombre.

Every time Bard looked into her eyes, he felt the aching, crushing burden of despair. Apart from the strong painkillers that she took regularly, the only thing that seemed to alleviate her suffering was Bard's voice. Her son's music calmed her down and gave her some comfort, even a little. A few days before her death, she put her hand on the cheek of her darling son and said in a barely audible whisper, "No matter where I am, know that whenever you sing a song, I'll be listening to you." She took her hand away from his cheek and placed it over his heart. "Look for me in here if you ever miss me, because here is where eternity lies and I'm forever there with you."

Bard was no longer able to contain his tears after his mother's words; he took Angela's hand and placed a thousand kisses on it. "I love you, Mum."

When Angela's big beautiful eyes closed for the last time, she had a peaceful smile on her face. She looked as if she was in a deep sleep filled with beautiful dreams; her expression remained unchanged for two days, after which she gave her last breath.

It was not easy for Bard. It was not easy to lose one's mother at only sixteen, so abruptly as well, in just three months. Bard loved his mother dearly; Angela was the pillar of his life; her death was surely going to affect him and it was not going to be easy to recover from this desolation. Thus, Bard withdrew into himself. He tried to ease the pain through music; it was the only remedy he knew. He took out his guitar whenever he could, strummed and sang tirelessly.

He thought music brought him closer to her, connecting the two souls in a mystical way. He knew deep in his soul that his mother heard him, that she was listening.

After Angela's untimely death, the bond between Bard and his father, Richard, which was already weak, was almost completely cut off. The two men withdrew to their separate worlds. Both, in their own distinct ways, were trying to find a way to cope with and overcome the melancholy inside.

Angela had always been the one to take care of the house as well as the needs of his young son. She was resourceful, practical and organised. She had an instinctive ability to communicate; it was easy to talk to her. Her deep gaze would capture you without realisation, cocoon you with affection and you would soon be left astounded as to how quickly you opened up to her. Bard admired this trait of hers, and of course, due to this ability, his mother became his best companion with whom he shared all his feelings, thoughts and problems since he was little.

Richard was a quiet man; he was devoted to his family. He loved his wife and son yet struggled with showing his fondness. That was one of the reasons why he felt so lucky to have Angela. He was the breadwinner but thanks to Angela he never once had to think about anything else other than work. He would often come home tired after a long day's work and fall asleep on the couch after dinner. Although he worked in the whiskey distillery, he was not fond of alcohol and would only drink a pint of beer once in a while when he was out with friends.

However, when the life in which he felt safe and content fell to pieces with the death of his wife Angela, Richard resorted to the ephemeral solace of alcohol, which was the only and most easily available comfort he knew. He drank every night, diving into the depths of drunken apathy. He started to come home late, drunk out of his mind, and passed out as soon as he made it inside.

Bard was aware that his father was not able to cope with his pain and was abusing alcohol as an escape from his sorrow. He also knew that he couldn't bear to step in a home where his wife wasn't in anymore. But Bard was still there. He was lonely as well; he had lost someone special to him as well; he needed his father. Of course, no one would be able to make up for his mother's absence; still he needed a branch, however weak and fragile, to hold on to in this sweeping emptiness. Luckily, he had his passion for music... Still, he was not sure for how long this passion would be able to shelter him. What if there were other traumas that he would have to face, what if he got once again drifted to unknown shores of sorrow; would this passion of his keep him company through what was to come?

Chapter 10

IN THE SUMMER BEFORE HIS LAST YEAR IN SECONDARY school, Bard started to work as a waiter in the restaurant owned by Sean's family, where he had also worked the summer before. He wanted to save as much money as he could before he went to university, so as not to be a burden to his father. He was able to save quite a lot last summer.

Sean was also helping out in the restaurant. The two of them had fun working together and when they were done with their shifts, they practised music. They had gotten even more ambitious ever since Mr O'Canon had told them that they could play for the customers from time to time.

As Bard took advantage of the restaurant being empty and started strumming his guitar pensively, his mind was occupied with the thought of that girl whom he saw frequently these days and who dazzled him more and more with each sight. She would come to the restaurant sometimes with her family and sometimes with her friends. The blondish strands in her light brown hair that flowed over her shoulders, shone like the sun with every movement of her gentle figure. The big almond-shaped eyes on her slender face, shed a honey-like glow when she smiled which radiated through the whole room. Bard was bewitched as soon as she entered through the door; the whole world stopped moving except his heart racing in a frenzied rush. He came across the girl outside the restaurant a few times; she smiled at him, but he just froze in his place and couldn't muster the courage to approach her.

"If you keep staring and don't get a move on soon, you will still be daydreaming when the summer is over. I don't know what you are waiting for, she obviously likes you," Sean scolded him; to which Bard replied by saying, "I guess you're right, but I am not confident when it comes to speaking with women, you know? I mean, other than my mother... I don't know how to act, more importantly, I don't even know if I want to have that close connection with someone. What if I do something wrong and lose her completely...?"

Looking into his friend's worry-ridden eyes, Sean said, "When we share loving memories with somebody, those memories stay with us; even if we lose our loved ones, what we shared remains ours forever. Isn't that better than having no memories at all?"

Bard looked up when the tiny bell over the door rang, signalling someone was entering through the doorway. After rubbing his eyes, which were dazed from the bright light coming in the dimly lit restaurant, he caught the sight of the girl approaching him with a smile. She greeted him, bowing with her head as she walked with her hands behind her.

"Hello, I hope I am not bothering you."

Befuddled, Bard dropped his guitar as he tried to stand up. He tried to stall for time in order to gain control over his emotions as he picked up the guitar and leaned it against the wall. When he turned his face to the girl, blood rushed to his cheeks. He scratched his head as he glanced shyly.

"Hi."

The warmth of her gaze set Bard aflame when the girl extended her hand to shake his. "My name is Maidie."

When their hands joined, a spark of heat shocked them both. Their eyes locked, hypnotised; Bard was barely able to make a sound. "I'm Bard."

"Oh, like those bards from the medieval times?"

Bard was surprised that she knew about it. "I think so. My mother was the one who named me. How did you know about its meaning?"

"I read it somewhere. I got interested in druids while I was researching the history of this place. They valued music, poetry and art; they also practised magic and healing. I heard the name Bard while I was reading about them."

"Wow, you really do know a lot about them!" said Bard with admiration. He was thinking, *She is as smart as she is beautiful*, when he realised his rudeness; he showed her to a seat.

"Would you like to sit down and have a drink?"

"No, thank you, I actually have to go soon, my father is waiting. I just stopped by to say something."

Maidie had worked out that this boy, whom she liked, was not going to approach her if she didn't take the first step, so she had decided to act. She took a deep breath. "Well… Tomorrow we are going to go to Staffa with some friends to visit Fingal's Cave. You could come with us, if you don't have any other plans."

Bard admired Maidie's courage as well as her beauty and intelligence. She had done what he couldn't bring himself to do. How lucky he was!

"Super! Of course, I'll definitely join you."

Maidie expected the boy to accept her offer, but still wasn't entirely sure. With his positive response, her tense shoulders relaxed and the cloudy expression in her eyes was replaced by a warm, sunny gleam.

"You can bring friends if you want, we have enough space."

"I may bring Sean."

Maidie looked towards the door. "I have to go now. We'll meet at the docks at nine in the morning tomorrow then."

Looking directly into her eyes, Bard replied, "I'll definitely be there, Maidie." He emphasised her name deliberately as he enjoyed the way it rolled off his tongue.

Maidie responded similarly. "See you, Bard."

Sean came in just as Maidie was leaving; he greeted her on his way. Then he approached his friend, raising an eyebrow with a mischievous smirk. "Judging by the silly expression on your face, I'm assuming that finally there is some progress."

"Uh huh…" Bard woke up from his reverie to respond to his friend in full sentences. "Yeah! Get ready, we're hanging out with our new friends tomorrow."

That night, Bard could not sleep a wink due to excitement. He kept turning in bed and checking the time. When he was finally able to fall asleep, he had the most curious dream. He was walking hand in hand with Maidie in the countryside, laughing and dancing. The strange part was Angela was also in his dream; she anxiously watched over them. It did not make much sense to Bard.

He was whistling chirpy tunes like a bird while he was getting ready to go out in the morning. He was walking on air as he and Sean made their way to the meeting spot. Sean, struggling to keep up with him, tried in vain to slow him down, saying, "Hey, slow down, the girl's not going to go anywhere!"

The two had arrived at the harbour before the others and noticed that the sea was slightly choppy. The air was dusted with grey clouds, and the greyness reflected on the sea. The gently blowing wind did not seem like it would make the clouds disperse soon. Except for one boat sailing far away, most of the boats were anchored near the harbour, slowly rising and falling with the waves.

Soon, Maidie and her two friends joined them. After they all met, they boarded the boat with the captain's help. The white wooden boat was small, but there was enough room for it to not feel too crowded. Once they were seated in the glass cabin, they all started to chat cheerfully as the little boat made its way through the waves.

As the boat moved away from the harbour, the turbulence of the sea increased, and the weather got even rougher. The young people in the cabin were unaware of the situation for quite a while, until the captain warned, "Children, as you can see, conditions are not exactly ideal. We might not be able to moor near the island, but we'll see if you're lucky." Although he was an experienced captain, he did not want to risk causing any harm to these young people; after all, it was mainly his responsibility. He called out to them without taking his eyes off the path ahead. "I could give you information about the island and the cave if you wish."

"It would be great," Maidie said, as she turned to see the approving faces of her friends.

They were all ears, as the captain started to speak loudly. "This place is estimated to be sixty million years old."

They mouthed 'ooh' all at once.

"It consists of hexagonal columns of basalt. The waves hitting the rocks outside and the echoes of the water flowing in offer a magnificent spectacle of sound for the visitors."

It showed from the brightening of his face as he talked, that the captain really adored the place. "Historically, it also has a mystical significance. The name of this place in the old Celtic language is 'an Uaimh Binn', which means 'the Melody Cave'. Druids believed that 'bards', the poets of that period, would end up developing special talents after they had visited the cave. Perhaps the silvery lyrics of those poets who had lived and visited the cave hundreds of years ago, are still echoing in the melody of this place."

Maidie jolted excitedly. "There's a Bard here." She turned to face him and exclaimed, "Maybe the echoes of the past will have an effect on you as well; you might acquire some mystical abilities."

Bard shook his head in embarrassment. "I'm sure I'm not one of them."

The captain, delighted that the young people were listening to him with interest and curiosity, continued, "This location had been famous since the ancient times. Authors such as Jules Verne, Tennyson and Queen Victoria were among its visitors. After visiting the cave and falling in love with its melody, Felix Mendelssohn was inspired to compose the *Fingal's Cave Overture*."

While proudly recounting the information on the place, the captain felt the need to stop and warn his eager young listeners to avoid any disappointment. "You may not be able to get off the boat and go ashore, though. Sometimes it is impossible to approach the island altogether."

When they reached Staffa, the strong wind and rough waves cradled the boat; their sight flickered between the foamy white surging sea and the cold greyness of the sky. The captain was holding on to the rudder of the boat firmly, trying to minimise the rocking of the boat. The passengers' faces turned green; their stomachs were turning. Everyone on the boat felt utterly dejected.

"Unfortunately, children, we cannot harbour at the island under these conditions. I will try to approach the entrance of the cave as much as possible. I'm sorry, but you'll have to do with what you can see from afar."

No one could raise an objection since their fears overcame their disappointment. They were sitting still, not moving an inch, and observing their surroundings with anxious glances.

As they drew nearer to the entrance of the cave, Bard's nausea grew more and more unbearable, and when they finally got there it was no longer possible to hold back. He threw himself out the passenger cabin before the captain could intervene. He leaned over the railing and vomited into the sea. They were right at the mouth of the cave. The waves rushing inside the cave were smacking into those that were gushing out, and as tides ripped, they created a whirlpool, which sucked the water in and birthed new waves. Bard was not relieved. Instead the chaos made him feel even dizzier; he couldn't stand up. With one last strike of the waves, before he could even understand what was going on, he found himself plunged in the water. The riptide wasted no time and the sea sucked him deeper.

His friends started screaming as they saw him falling overboard.

Everyone climbed onto the deck of the boat, shouting from all sides, trying to make their voices heard and to catch sight of him. The captain, who was not able to leave the rudder, shouted his instructions from there. "Hold tight! I don't want anyone else falling."

Just then, Sean shouted, pointing his finger towards the entrance of the cave, "I saw his head, he's going in."

"Is there a good swimmer amongst you? Whoever it is should just put on a life jacket and jump. I can't get the boat any closer to him."

Sean was already wearing his life jacket.

"Take that lifebuoy as well – come on, quick. Watch out for the rocks!"

As Sean jumped into the water and swam into the cave, miraculously the sea calmed down. The waves were suddenly restful as if they had accomplished their duty. The sea surface was still wavy, yet these were small and orderly. When Sean noticed a flat rock and climbed onto it, he noticed that the others, wearing their lifejackets, had disembarked as well, thanks to the extraordinary efforts of the captain in approaching the island. They were moving closer to where Sean was and shouting Bard's name. Their voices echoed from the walls of the cave, mingling with the centuries-old melodies; it was as if thousands of voices were calling Bard's name.

Maidie was the first to see Bard. A glimmer of hope appeared in her fearful eyes as she shouted, "Look, look at the edge of that high and flat rock over there!"

They all ran towards that direction. Bard was lying on his stomach, unconscious. Sean immediately knelt down next to him, grabbed his shoulders and turned him around. As he put his finger on the vein on his neck, he was muttering to himself deliriously, "Please, God, please don't take him from us!"

Bard's eyelids trembled open as he heard his name; however, his gaze was empty and senseless.

Meanwhile, the captain, who had finally managed to anchor the boat, hurried near them. He put his hand on Bard's neck, lifted his head and slightly shook it. "Are you okay, son?"

Bard's voice was barely audible. "I'm fine."

"Come on then, we need to get going before we push our luck any further."

When the captain made a move to lift him in his arms, Bard struggled to escape his hold. As he shouted, "Let me go!", his gaze was strange, like he didn't recognise those around him.

Sean moved nearer to his friend. "Bard, it's me, your friend. Come on, try to pull it together, we have to leave the island as soon as possible."

Maidie spoke tearfully as he held his hand. "Try to inhale and exhale slowly, deep breaths. Please try to collect yourself. You're safe now."

Bard followed her advice and slowly gathered his breath; colour came back to his face. His eyes assumed their usual look and he slowly slipped out of his dazed state. When they sat him up, he was fully conscious. It felt as if he had just travelled through dimensions. There was nothing wrong with him physically, but his mind was all muddled. He had experienced some bizarre, very bizarre things.

He nodded when the captain asked, "Can you stand up?"

The man wrapped his arm around under his shoulders, supported his weight and helped him walk. When he got on the boat, he first helped Bard and then the rest of the kids to safely come aboard. He gave them a towel and some dry clothes of his, then quickly set sail back to Tobermory.

"You were lucky – or more like we all were. You could get hypothermia in such weather, in such freezing waters. Thank goodness you're fine!"

After the terrifying and straining incident, everyone felt that the return journey dragged on for too long. Was the air colder? Was the sky a darker grey? It was not just Bard who was shaking under the blanket he was wrapped in; all of them trembled with the impact of the trauma.

Bard gradually recovered; by the time they arrived in Tobermory, the haziness in his eyes had dispersed and his cheeks were back to their natural colour. When they got out of the boat, he did not physically show any impacts regarding the incident. Despite everyone's insistence, he refused to go to the hospital.

"I'm all right, I'm just cold. If I could warm myself up and rest a little bit, I would be completely fine."

They left after thanking the captain. Along with Sean, Maidie and her friends insisted on accompanying Bard to his home. Maidie lingered on a bit more after they all said their goodbyes; when she was the last one there, she reached out and took his hand. "I'm worried about you. Please let me know if you feel worse."

Bard, who was beginning to warm up under her mellow gaze, finally said goodbye to her, promising to call if anything went wrong. He didn't let Sean stay, either. He put on his own clothes and went straight to bed, pulling the duvet over his head and waiting for the heat to accumulate as the visions of the strange underwater occurrence and anxious questions filled his mind. He had an uncomfortable night with strange nightmares.

When Sean arrived with freshly baked bread in hand, Bard had just woken up and was trying to come to his senses. They had their breakfast in silence. Sean was afraid to talk and to ask about what happened yesterday. How did he survive? He must have been underwater for more than five minutes; breathless for five minutes! It was freezing cold to top it off; this was a complete miracle!

Sean was lost in thought when he heard Bard's voice. Bard was leaning back on the faded navy-blue sofa; his eyes were glued to the ceiling. "I suddenly lost my balance as I was throwing up. The moment I fell into the water, I got caught in the riptide. I couldn't move. I just sank deeper and deeper into the whirling water. At first, I was surrounded by the whiteness of the waves and sea foam, but soon it all got pitch dark and the ringing noises in my ears slowly ceased. I felt like an object floating about in the void of outer space, in total darkness, weightless. I couldn't feel anything anymore."

He continued after filling his lungs with a deep inhale. "At that moment, a rainbow of light appeared within the darkness, shining towards me like a shooting star; it took me in and pulled me up; then it laid me on that rock in the cave. It gave me breath, filled me in, travelling from my mouth to my lungs and then to all the tissues of my being, to my whole body. It was incredibly calming, like a soft melody..."

Sean was listening intently with eyes wide open; he was barely breathing so as not to distract his friend from telling his story.

"When I opened my eyes, there was a bright and gorgeous fairy in front of me. Her transparent skin was dazzling with the light of thousands, millions of tiny sea sparkles. She radiated rainbow colours. The only darkness in all of her glow was her big black eyes. They were deep and fathomless; just like black holes in outer space. I must have passed out, gazing into them. I woke up with your voice."

He let out a deep sigh as he was done speaking. "So, here's the story; it is bizarre and hard to believe." He glanced straight at Sean without lifting his head; his eyes were full of concern. "What do you think? Do you think I'm losing my mind or was it all a hallucination?"

Sean looked at him, scratching his head. "I don't know what to say. It was certainly a miracle, but it is not easy to believe all that you are telling me right now. It is strange. Then, you know, the cave itself apparently is a mystical place."

"Maybe I died and was resurrected, huh?" Bard suddenly shifted to face Sean and sat with one leg under him and stared fixedly.

"I know it's bizarre. I cannot make sense of it either, that's why we must keep this as a secret between us, okay? Nobody needs to know, including my father. Though I bet he sees far more mysterious visions when he loses his senses under the influence."

He looked away with a bitter grin. "Do you know what's weird about it?"

"What?"

"I feel full of energy. I feel at peace. The strangeness of what happened does not bother me. It is both unsettling and comforting."

Sean was worried about his friend. The things he was saying were not at all normal. Could he be suffering from a concussion or some sort of brain damage due to the prolonged lack of oxygen? *I must convince him to go to the doctor somehow*, he thought, distraught.

Bard continued to speak, his unusual mood reflecting in his tone. "That wasn't even the whole of it. I have more to say. I saw that fairy from yesterday in my dream. I was hearing a mystical, divine melody that came from afar, from a void. Then the fairy appeared in all her radiance and she spoke in a comforting, magical voice as she said that she gave me a special gift. She then vanished before I could ask what it was."

Sean gave a small jab in his friend's shoulder. "I think the water diluted your brain yesterday." He was joking but deep down he was really worried. "I think you should see a doctor, just in case. You may not have physical damage, but you may be experiencing some psychological trauma."

The conversation ended with a knock on the door. It was Maidie. Her large hazel eyes opened wider with concern. "I wondered if you were feeling okay."

Bard opened the door widely and stepped aside to let her in. He combed his hair back with his fingers and smiled. "I'm fine, thank you. Do you want to sit down?"

Meanwhile, Sean appeared beside them with a mischievous grin on his face. "Hello, Maidie, I'm glad you're here, I had some things to attend to. I'll just hand our patient over to your care."

When they were alone, they were both seized by excitement. After a brief silence, Bard gestured to the table he had just been sitting at with Sean.

"Here," he said as he began to clear the breakfast plates.

Maidie jerked up just as she was sitting down. "Can I help you?"

"No, no. Please sit down. I'll just put these in the kitchen and come join you."

When Bard returned to sit down beside her, Maidie clasped her hands and put them in between her knees; her cheeks turned pink. "I couldn't sleep last night thinking about you."

Her words melted Bard's heart. He felt his entire soul being pulled towards her as he responded with a soft voice. "You lost sleep over nothing. Believe me, I was feeling alright."

Maidie's glassy eyes shifted from hazel to green; her lips were trembling slightly. "I'm glad. I would have never forgiven myself if something had happened to you. I wish we never went there."

Bard reached out and grabbed her chin, lifted her head and looked deeply into her eyes. "No, don't say that. I came voluntarily, and it was my fault to dangle from the railing like I did. No one else is at fault here, so please don't be upset, okay?"

Maidie pressed her lips together and nodded. When her eyes started to sparkle like before, Bard was captivated by the beauty of her gaze. The tension in the air made them both uneasy.

Maidie tucked her hair behind her ear and spoke shyly. "Anyway! I'll go now."

The two stood up at the same time.

When Maidie reached the door, Bard gathered his courage after briefly hesitating. "What are you doing tomorrow? Do you have any plans?"

The girl's face lit up with excitement. "No, I don't."

"How about going on a bike ride?" he said, then added with a smirk, "It's less dangerous."

"I think it is a great idea."

The next day, before meeting up with Maidie, Bard wanted to go to the O'Canon restaurant a little earlier to see Sean. When he got there, his friend was laying the tablecloths. He approached him with a spring in his step.

"You look good, mate, what is up with the whole fairy thing?"

Bard was grinning wide. "Forget about that, I'm good, I'll be meeting up with Maidie now.

Sean frowned and his face took on a mock expression of anger. "So, you're ditching me to be with your girl, huh? That must be the reason for that silly expression on your face."

Seeing Maidie coming towards them through the window, Bard hurriedly patted Sean's shoulder. "I'm out, see you."

As the girl got off her bike, Bard watched her, thinking, *She looks fresh like a spring breeze.*

Maidie didn't seem to notice the effect she had on Bard when the sunlight danced through her hair. "Hey! Hello, am I late?"

"No, no. I was just here early." He pulled on the straps on his chest and straightened his backpack.

"Well, where are we going?"

"You choose, is there a place you'd like to see?"

Maidie thought, squinting her eyes. "Actually, there is. I want to take you to a place I love very much."

Bard motioned as if he is saluting a soldier. "Aye aye, lead the way, please."

After a merry journey of twenty minutes through the narrow, winding roads of the lush green countryside, they got off their bikes and took in the view from the top. Today, the sea was bluer. As the sunlight hit the small waves created by the gentle wind, the sea twinkled with the flicker of its reflection. Maidie pointed down with excitement; anticipation shone in her eyes as she showed him her favourite beach. Bard turned to her when he saw the tiny white beach among the rocks, which was not visible at first glance but could be seen as one drew nearer.

"Wow! It's secluded. One could run away from everything and hide up here. How did you discover this place? I'm from here and still I have never noticed this little shore before."

"My dad discovered it. He's a zoology professor. When the school breaks up for summer, we head straight to Tobermory. He is doing research here; I help him too sometimes." She continued, pointing ahead. "There. Do you see that pile of moss and twigs? Otters go there to rest sometimes. If we wait patiently, and of course, if we're lucky, we might be able to see them."

Bard remarked cheekily, "I think I am quite lucky."

They descended the curved path cautiously, smiling all the way down. They sat on a wide rock at the end of the beach, a little further from the sea. Maidie took a long deep breath, looked around and took in the view, then she lifted her face to the sky, closed her eyes and enjoyed the warm sunlight on her skin. Bard reclined back on his elbows as he watched her in admiration.

"What is your father's research on?"

Maidie opened her eyes slightly as she also took a more recumbent position, leaning back on her hands. "He is exploring the wildlife in the area. He compiles information and conveys it to the university he is affiliated with, as well as various journals and institutions who are interested in wildlife preservation."

"It must be a pleasant occupation; it sure sounds interesting."

Maidie was flattered by Bard's attention. "His research covers all the animals in the region. Sea eagles, dolphins, puffins…"

Bard sat up and wrapped his arms around his knees. He noticed the delight in Maidie's voice as she talked about it. He was dying to get to know her better, to learn about her interests and share her passions. "So, what do you think you will do in the future?"

Determination was evident in her every move as she lifted her chin and straightened her shoulders. "I'm going to study veterinary medicine… My dad observes animals from afar, whereas I'd like to be much closer. I'd like to have an opportunity to connect with them."

"Sounds wonderful! I am sure you will be a very good veterinarian."

"What about you?"

"My goal is to be a good musician, the best I can. I want to get an education and have a career in music." Like Maidie, his determination was reflected in his gaze.

"You play the guitar, right?"

"Yes, my guitar is a part of me." His squinted eyes wandered about in search of the right words to express his thoughts for a while; he then continued, "I don't know how to explain, but making music brings forth a divine emotion. It gives me peace. When I let the music in me play out on my guitar or my song, I feel incredibly calm and content."

Maidie stared at him admiringly. "Wow, you are so passionate about it. I would love to listen to your music sometime."

"With pleasure, whenever you want…"

Just then, they noticed the swashing of the sea. Maidie brought her finger to her lips to make a shushing gesture. "Do you see it? Oh my, I can't believe it, it has a baby in its arms." Her eyes sparkled as she glanced gleefully at Bard. "Isn't it great?"

It was a sight worth seeing: the mother otter was swimming on her back and carrying her baby on her chest. As Bard marvelled at the fascinating and rare sight in front of him, his mind was also occupied with thoughts of Maidie. She was gorgeous with a sincere, pure demeanour; it was impossible not to fall for her.

After chatting for a few hours and getting to know each other a little more, it was time to go back. Bard took Maidie's hand and helped her get up. They shook the dust off their clothes, started climbing up the path and made their way to the road above the hill.

When they got on their bikes, Bard flashed a defiant smirk. "Ready for a race?"

Instead of answering him, Maidie cranked the pedals and hurried down the road. "Okay," she called out to Bard, whom she'd left behind, with laughter.

When they arrived at the town centre, bursting with giggles, Maidie, who was the winner of the race, was fanning herself, maintaining her balance with one foot on the ground.

"Don't think I've fallen for your little gimmick. I know that you were deliberately easy on me. Still it was nice to beat you."

Bard had gotten off his bike and was standing next to her. Before he knew it, he was struck dumb by a soft kiss on his cheek.

"Thank you, I had a lot of fun."

Stupefied with his hand on his blushing cheek, Bard said, "Thank you, it was an absolute pleasure. Should we repeat this tomorrow?"

"Okay. Same place, same time?"

After Maidie left, Bard walked to the restaurant treading on air. He felt light as a feather. When he got inside, he felt certain about his feelings. As his friend Sean approached him, he spoke with that intrinsic sureness: "I think I am in love. It is strange. I've never felt like this, I didn't even know that this feeling existed. I feel like I am seeing the world with brand-new eyes."

Sean smiled wide. "It sure is strange. I bet you'll grow a pair of wings and fly away soon."

Bard glanced around; the restaurant was empty. "Let's make some music, I feel a beautiful song surging inside my soul."

He took his guitar in his arms. At first, he started by playing a few notes but then the melodies started to flow out in ecstasy. Love, joy and happiness took form in his notes. When he was done, he put the guitar aside and said, with the peace of mind of being able to convey his emotions through song, "I'll call this one 'The Beginning.'" He didn't know where this song had come from; he was positively perplexed. Notes had never before come together so flawlessly. It felt like there was an endless source of melody inside his soul and the song just overflew.

Sean looked at him proudly. "That was truly wonderful. Whatever it is that inspires you, it sure is a great thing. I hope you'll have many more 'beginnings.'"

The next day, when he met with Maidie again, Bard's guitar was hanging from his shoulder.

The girl's eyes sparkled with joy. "Heyy! You brought your guitar, that's great."

Bard tapped the case on his shoulder. "I hope you'll like it; I don't want to embarrass myself trying to impress you."

She responded to his banter with similar sarcasm in her voice. "We'll see, I have to hear you first before saying anything. So today is your day, where are you going to take me?"

They got on their bikes and rode, sometimes side by side, sometimes back to back. They were tired from pedalling when they finally reached the beach where the white sand stretched as far as the eye could see. The foamy white waves were rushing to the shore like wild horses galloping across fields. Rainbows flickered between the mist of the waves crashing.

Bard smiled in delight. "This is my sanctuary. I can sit for hours and listen to the sound of the waves hitting the shore. This place makes me feel eternal, like I am a part of eternity."

Maidie got off her bike; she wasn't able to take her eyes off the view. "It really is fascinating."

With a smile, she held the hand that Bard was extending to her; together they walked through the greenery towards the white sandy shore. Maidie took out the blanket that she'd brought from her backpack and spread it out on the floor; they sat side by side. For a while they just listened to the sound of the waves without a word.

A while later, they were reclining on their elbows comfortably as they chatted about everything from their daily lives to their studies in school. Eventually, Maidie got up and sat down on her knees. "All right, it's time! Will you play for me now?"

"Your wish is my command, miss."

He took the guitar out of its case; after tuning a little, he started to play. He was bewildered by his own performance; he was not completely in control. His fingers moved with a mind of their own and the melody they produced was of outstanding beauty.

Maidie seemed to be enthralled as well. She had never heard such a touching, soulful melody before. Her eyes shone green, full of emotion. "You, you... This is awesome. I loved it, it's the first time I've ever heard of this song."

How was Bard ever going to explain what had just happened to him, when he couldn't even understand it himself... He did not understand where this melody had come from. He'd never played it before, nor had he heard it, yet he knew it by heart... He was actually quite scared by what had happened, yet he did not want to show it to Maidie.

"I've been working on it for a long time," he fibbed.

As the girl stared at him in awe, Bard felt as if he could see beyond these big beautiful eyes and into her soul. He sensed a magical pull towards her. He drew closer to her, put a hand on her cheek and, as their gazes locked, he muttered, "Your eyes are beautiful."

The girl smiled. "They change colours when they get wet."

Bard whispered, terrified of ruining the moment, "I just hope it's not only my music that you like."

His heart was almost going to leap out of his chest when he placed a small kiss on her lips. Their lips were almost still touching when he continued whispering, "I like you so much."

Maidie's cheeks flushed. "I like you too."

As their lips joined for a second time, their kiss was longer and more passionate. After they parted lips, they stood still for a while, watching the sea, drunk on each other's taste. The feeling made Bard forget the uneasiness caused by that melody which had come out of nowhere and took over his soul. This time he picked up his guitar to play something he already knew.

Maidie hugged her legs and leaned against her knees, facing Bard.

"There was an incredible intensity of emotion in your music," she said. "It echoed a certain sense of pain and despair – am I wrong?"

"I guess you are right. I composed this one while my mother was sick. She was really ill; she was in a lot of pain and we could do nothing to relieve it. I was so desperate…" Bard relived the past as he gazed into the distance with hazy eyes. "She loved listening to me. She wanted me to play and sing for hours every day, especially when her pain was unbearable." His voice had a tremble, along with his body, which was also shaking like a leaf.

As a single tear slowly rolled down his cheek, Maidie leaned over and wiped it away. "I'm sure your voice helped her through her pain. It has a tone to it that sparks of a feeling of comfort and peace."

Bard took in a deep breath. "That's enough gloom," he said as he started to strum the guitar strings once again and the melody of the song that he had composed yesterday flowed out by itself. As he was playing the song, he was surprised that he was able to remember all the notes to it.

The joyful, chirpy composition dispelled the dark clouds hovering over the two and a sunny, light-hearted mood lit up their faces. Maidie applauded excitedly when his song was finished.

"Don't ever stop making music. Your talent is exceptional and I'm sure you'll do great things in the future," she said, then she reached out and kissed him. They started out hesitant and shy but soon the kiss grew impassioned. With the wind picking up, they became more aware of their surroundings and realised that it was time to return, though they did not wish to. Bard took Maidie's hand and helped her up; they shook the sand off the blanket and placed it in the bag. As they walked hand in hand to their bikes, they both had hopes and dreams of a happy future. Still, Bard was confused about what had just happened as he was playing the guitar and was scared about the fact that things started to creep up on him without his control.

Although Bard kept having strange dreams about the fairy occasionally, he did not mind. The only thing that mattered in his life right now was

Maidie. They spent all their time together. They wanted to know more and more about each other and be able to see the world through each other's eyes.

Sean had a girlfriend as well now. He was dating Cordelia, whom he knew from school and he'd liked for a while. The four of them usually hung out together, exploring Tobermory, as well as themselves. Their days were fun and merry. Sometimes they would bring their guitars with them to sing and dance.

Sometimes, in moments where Bard surrendered to soul-stirring emotions, he would mutter the songs to Maidie's ears and she would say, "I can listen to you forever. Your voice is like an angel's whisper." In fact, he himself had noticed a certain change in the tone of his voice; his voice was unusually soft as velvet. There also had been another incident. He'd started strumming and singing all of a sudden again, playing a melody he had never heard before. All of these changes coincided with the accident in the Fingal's Cave, which made him think about all those legends about bards who visited the cave. Could they be real…?

That night, Bard had made a romantic dinner for Maidie. He made some spaghetti and set up a candle-lit table.

When Maidie came and saw his surprise, her eyes opened wide with joy. "You did all this for me?"

Bard, who was standing behind her, reached out to hug her and kissed her hair. "This was all I could do for now, but you deserve much better. You deserve the best of everything."

During the meal, they talked about their future plans. Then, they danced together to the songs that Bard was singing in whispers. Maidie was trembling as the melodies travelled through her ears and took over her whole body. Bard's whispers slowly turned into kisses. The tiny warm touches of his lips electrified her body. Maidie was filled by desire as the touches travelled to her neck then to her lips. When their lips met, sparks went off like lightning before a storm of passion. With the brush of skin, their hands wandered to discover more of each other and every discovery set them aflame even more.

Bard hoisted himself up on his elbow as they lay snuggling on the wrinkled, sweat-soaked sheet. His loving gaze was shadowed with worry. "Did I hurt you? Do you regret it?"

Maidie shifted towards him, reached out and grabbed his cheek. She had a tired but content smile. "I'm glad that I experienced this with you. I love you."

Bard was happy to hear all that; he grabbed her face with both hands and gave her a kiss. "I love you too, I love you so very much."

After that night, they continued discovering each other's bodies, sometimes under the stars, sometimes in Bard's room, sometimes on the beach, trying to smother the fire of their young love with the cool waters of desire.

They had many plans for the future. They wanted to attend the same university, share a house, travel a lot and explore new places and volunteer to protect natural life together... They were looking forward to the days they had dreamed about; they were full of hope and anticipation.

Everything was fine, yet Bard was not truly at peace. He was strangely uneasy. Although his mind told him not to be bothered by those dreams about the fairy, his intuitions told something different. Its effect increased day by day. "A special gift," she'd said – what was that? What should he make out of all that? Was it good or bad? The only thing he knew for sure was the growing uneasiness that captured his soul. Maybe his gift was those beautiful musical compositions that poured out of him? The thought brought him some relief.

The holidays were over in the blink of an eye. On the last day they had with each other, they sat side by side on the wooden bench, where they always sat; they stared at each other, with eyes as dull as the dim sunlight peeking lazily through the clouds.

"We don't live so far away from each other; we can meet up if we wish to. And I'll be here as soon as the school closes."

"You're right. If we want to attend the same university next year, we both should focus on our studies."

He stroked and kissed Maidie's hair. A new life was upon them, and it was going to be filled with joy and happiness, right...?

Chapter 11

MELISSA FELT LIKE SHE WAS HEARING ABOUT THE LIFE OF a stranger. These stories she was being told had nothing to do with the father she knew, or rather, she thought she knew. She was not sure what to say or what to think; her shocked gaze was dark and empty, not revealing the storms breaking in her soul. Sean noticed that the girl was quite shocked, so he thought it was time to take a break. He got up from his seat.

"My mouth is dry, I will make coffee, would anyone else like some?"

With great difficulty, Melissa's lips curled into a gentle smile. "Thank you, I'll just have some water, please."

As her husband made a move to prepare the coffee, Cordelia chipped in affectionately, "I'll do it, honey."

"Well, then I'll help you," Sean insisted, and followed her out the room. He sighed and murmured to his wife, "The poor girl looked shaken, I thought I should give her some space."

Meanwhile, William was quietly observing Melissa from the corner where he was sitting, trying to decipher her emotions. Though he thought that the girl must be upset, he decided to ignore it, so as not to hurt her pride by fawning over her.

When Sean got back to the living room with the tray in his hands, Melissa's eyes were emptily staring into the fireplace. She was startled by the sound of the door.

Sean offered her a glass of water with a kind and gentle look in his eyes. "I'm sorry, I didn't mean to scare you."

Melissa took the glass, shifted in her seat and sat down with her legs under her. "I got lost in thought for a second."

Sean sat back down in his armchair, careful so as not to spill the coffee in his hands. "Do you feel any better? Shall I continue?"

Melissa's eyes were as dark as the green moss deep in the shadowy corners of the sea. "I think I need some time." She then opened her mouth to say something but gave up. After briefly hesitating she continued to speak: "Do you think what happened in the cave was real? Or maybe it was due to some kind of a psychological issue he was having? Maybe it was the trauma of the incident?" In desperate curiosity, her gaze shifted in between the two men, hoping that they could guide her thoughts.

As William kept his silence, Sean placed his cup of coffee on the table and took a deep breath. "I cannot answer that. I can tell you the parts of the story that I know and maybe you will find your answers when I'm done."

Chapter 12

AUTUMN HAD ARRIVED; THE WHOLE WORLD WAS DRAPED in yellows, oranges and reds. Tobermory's natural landscape was now as colourful as its little houses. Trees gushed out in the backdrop of the colourful houses lined in parallel to the grey and blue sea. The foliage of different shades was almost fighting to attract the onlookers' attention, putting on amazing displays of beauty. The autumn here was a different kind of beautiful.

However, for Bard, it all meant nothing. Without Maidie, no sight seemed to please him. The things he used to love and cherish had all lost their charms when she was not around. His only wish was that the winter would be over soon and the summer holidays would start so he could see Maidie. They had exchanged letters frequently and written about how much they missed each other. Still, Bard had a secret that he kept from her, that he couldn't bring himself to say. The fairy who'd invaded his every dream ever since that unexplainable incident in Fingal's Cave. What was he going to say to her? How was he going to explain something even he himself didn't understand? Was he going to tell her that he was saved from drowning by a fairy, whom he'd kept dreaming about every night since then? Who would believe in such a fairy tale? It was best to let it go and wait for it to pass. These dreams were going to end sooner or later anyway...

Bard would go to school on weekdays and work at the O'Canon restaurant on weekends. He was saving as much money as he could for the university. Though he was hoping to secure a scholarship by working hard and keeping his grades high, the plans he'd made with

Maidie meant that there was going to be some additional costs, so he thought it was better to grind away now than fall into trouble later. Plus, with his busy pace, the time passed much quicker.

On that rainy Saturday, Cedric O'Canon greeted Bard enthusiastically when he entered the restaurant. "Ah! Good thing you came early. We are short on kitchen supplies; I need to go shopping now."

"I'll go for you if you want."

Meanwhile, Cedric took off his apron and put on his coat. "No, I need to choose the groceries myself. I'm leaving the shop to you for now. I'll be back soon."

When he was alone, Bard looked around for a second, then he started by laying the tablecloths. He set the tables and tidied up the bar counter. He must have spent quite some time busying away. He felt a strange sense of discomfort; his heart was heavy. Suddenly he heard the whisper of the fairy rising from within his soul. "Sing my song," she uttered. He collapsed on a chair, pale-faced and short of breath. With the shrill sound of the ringing phone, he jumped up with a small shriek. It was Mrs O'Canon calling. She sounded downcast. "Bard, honey, Cedric was in an accident, we're in the hospital right now."

He was frozen in place with the weight of this information; he asked in a mutter, though he was scared to hear the answer, "Is he okay?"

"He is, darling, he is okay. He just has a few fractured bones. Would you be kind enough to find Sean and let him know? Oh, and also, close down the restaurant and put a note on the door explaining the situation."

Bard was locking the door, dazed by both the whisper he had heard and the news he had received, when Sean appeared behind him without Bard needing to look for him. When Sean saw the note on the door, his face went chalk-white and his eyes widened in fear. Bard told him all he knew as quick as possible in the hope that it may give him some reassurance. As Sean was getting ready to get on his bike, Colin, one of his father's friends, was approaching them. When he learned about the accident, the man offered to drive them to the hospital. Sean refused to believe that his father was okay until they arrived at the hospital; throughout the drive he looked out from the car window with tears raining down his cheeks.

They were relieved when they finally got to the hospital. Yes, he did have some fractured bones, but there wasn't anything that wouldn't heal. As he was rushing back from the supermarket, Cedric had slipped on the wet, leaf-covered floor and fell down four steps on the stairs. As his hands were full, he wasn't able to hold on to keep his balance. His right arm was broken in two places, his ankle was injured and they had to stitch up his eyebrow. He seemed to be untroubled as he was under the influence of painkillers. The family let out a sigh of relief, thankful that they were all together, while Bard watched from a distance. When he heard the whispers once more, he trembled with fear. The fairy was now whispering a beautiful, moving melody. Apart from his dreams, he had never experienced such a strange phenomenon as this.

When Sean turned to look at him, he noticed that something was wrong. "Hey! Are you okay? You look like you've seen a ghost."

The voices inside his head were growing louder and he was having a hard time connecting with the world outside. There was only him and the fairy now. He could only come to his senses when Sean grabbed his arms and shook him. His voice was weak. "I'm fine, I'm fine. I think the smell of medicine is giving me a headache."

Mrs O'Canon realised that the boy must have spent a lot of time at hospitals during his mother's illness and said, "Come on, children, you should return home. There is not much to do here anyway. We shouldn't keep Colin waiting as well, he's hanging around so that he could take you back."

Sean was going to stay at Bard's. They went straight home and holed themselves up in Bard's room.

Bard sat down on the bed, with a pen and paper in his hand and his guitar on his lap. "Let me just get this song off my mind first, then we'll talk," he said as he strummed and transcribed the music. When he was done, he lifted his head and the confused glances of the two kids met. Bard laid the guitar on the bed.

Sean rubbed his tired face in frustration; he had no patience left. "Yes, go on, tell me. What's going on! You are acting really weird, you're scaring me."

Hunkering down with his elbows on his knees, Bard was looking down as he held his head in his hands. He sounded anxious. "I don't understand it either. I heard a whisper today for the first time just before your mother called to tell me about the accident, right when the phone rang. Then, at the hospital, the fairy whispered for the second time; she sang me the song I just played." He drew his fingers through his hair and tugged. "Oh! I think I'm going crazy." He had his fist over his heart as he uttered, "You know, despite the fear, I still have a sense of serenity in my heart."

Sean sat in front of his friend and put his hands on his shoulders, looking at him. "If someone whispered such a sweet melody in my ear, I reckon I'd be feeling at peace as well."

Bard grabbed the arms extending over his shoulders. "I think this is the gift the fairy was talking about. But I don't understand why I would be the one to be bestowed such a gift. Maybe it would have been you if you were the one who fell to the sea."

Sean sat up straight, and he looked firm and determined. "No, I don't think so. I don't have your ability in music. It is nothing compared to your unique talent and velvety voice. You are already fascinating even when singing an ordinary song, but when you play such divine music, it is truly out of this world. Whatever it is that is happening, it's something special; it is a good thing, Bard, very good."

"I hope so. Anyway... Maybe it was a one-time thing, maybe it won't happen again. This might all be a coincidence."

However, this was not going to be the only time, nor it was going to be the last. It was just the beginning.

～

As winter was in full swing, Bard was spending most of his days focusing on his schoolwork and studying at home. He didn't go out much except for school and going for his weekend shifts at the restaurant. He wasn't even interested in music these days.

The day had passed just like the other day: he studied a little after the dinner that he had by himself and dreamt of Maidie as he lay on his bed. It has been a long time since he had stopped waiting for his father to come home in the evenings. If he wanted to hide in that little pub and drink to forget, then he was welcome to do so.

He was just dozing off when he woke up to a loud noise. It must have been his father, he thought, who had gotten drunk again and tripped over something or knocked something over. However, at that instance, the fairy's voice reached his ears once again. It was whispering the same words: "Sing my song." Distressed, he got up, opened the door and listened to hear a groan coming from his father's room. When he rushed in, he found him on the ground, unconscious. He did not seem well at all. Not knowing what to do, Bard shook him a little to bring him around, but it did not make a difference. He ran out in a frenzy and called Doctor James. After a quick inspection, it was established that he needed to be driven to a hospital as quickly as possible.

The medical examinations revealed that he'd had a severe heart spasm. Bard listened with his stomach in knots as the doctor explained, "It is miraculous for a patient to survive such a severe attack – what happened tonight was a true miracle."

Bard could not stop trembling.

The doctor smiled slightly and held his shoulders. "Relax now, your father will recover thanks to your quick response. He is lucky that you were around, kid. Your father owes his life to you."

As the doctor walked away, Bard leaned against the wall and closed his eyes. His trembles subsided as he muttered to himself, "He's fine, he'll be fine." He felt grateful for the fairy. If he hadn't heard its whisper, he wouldn't have sensed that there was something wrong, he wouldn't have listened, he wouldn't have heard his groans and his father would probably not be alive. The thought unsettled him. He had no one but his father; he couldn't bear to lose him too. Cedric's accident came to his mind. The whisper had foretold that incident as well. If only he had known of the fairy while his mother was still alive. Maybe… Maybe then, his mother would have survived too.

He started to transcribe the song of the fairy as soon as he got back home, with questions flooding his mind: *Is it always going to be like this? Is the whisper of the fairy always going be an omen of bad things to come, helping me turn my pain into melodies? Is this my gift?* He couldn't ponder any longer as he was overwhelmed with exhaustion. He fell asleep as soon as he curled up in his bed.

After passing through the hospital corridors drenched in chemical stench, he reached his father's room. He was happy to see that he was fine, despite the IV tube on his arm, the various cables draped all over him and the shrill of the annoying beeping of the monitor attached to his heart. His father was able to notice Bard enter through the door, as the back of his bed was slightly raised. His pink cheeks were a harbinger of good health. His gaze was bright, though this might have been due to his teary eyes. As Bard approached the bed and grabbed his hand, a teardrop escaped from his eyes. "Son," he said, all his fear, longing and love translated into one word, "I scared you."

Bard's tears flowed quiet and warm on his cheeks; he sniffed as he wiped his face with his free hand. "No, Dad, I was just worried, that's all. You are strong, I knew you'd survive this." He wasn't sure whether he was saying these words to console his father or himself.

Bard walked away from the bed when the doctor came into the room. His full-toned voice matched the appearance of this burly, grey-haired man in his sixties. After he checked the monitor and the follow-up file, he gave some instructions to the nurse beside him, then turned his gaze to Richard. "Everything seems fine, but we will keep you here today as a precaution. We will re-evaluate tomorrow," he said with a courteous nod and left.

When they were alone in the room, Richard was looking at his son with a tender heart. "I left you alone, you were so lonely. I know I wasn't good to you, but I promise I'll change. I'll be a different person when I get out of here..." His father raised his hand to interrupt him when Bard opened his mouth to speak. "Let me finish. In that moment when I thought I was going to die, the only thing that crossed my mind was you; I was afraid of leaving you all alone in this world." He licked his drying lips and continued, "Then I realised that I already abandoned you, while I'm still alive. I'm sorry, my son, I love you." As he ended his words, both were in tears.

Two days later, when Richard was discharged, on the first day that he returned home, a new life began for the two of them. They felt like they were a family again and they were happy to have each other. They realised once again that every day one can spend with loved ones is a gift and that they should be thankful for it.

Chapter 13

Ever since Richard had regained his health, he had kept to his word and changed his ways. He came home as soon as he left work and he hadn't touched a drop of alcohol. They had their meals together, telling each other about their day, talking about their lives. His father appreciated and supported Bard's flair for music. From time to time, he played songs that he wrote for his mother or the songs that she liked, to revisit the memories of her. They no longer concealed their emotions. 'Happiness shared is doubled and sadness shared is halved,' was their new belief. Occasionally, they would visit Angela's grave and decorate it with flowers. Although she was not with them physically, they both felt her presence and knew that her soul was at peace. Thinking about what he had missed as his son grew up to be a young man and about how lonely he must have felt through these two years broke Richard's heart; he was now trying harder to make up for all that. Bard, on the other hand, often thought, *How strange us humans are – we only value the precious things in our life when we lose them and we only acknowledge the good once we've seen the bad.*

During a conversation about the beautiful things in life, Bard mentioned Maidie. His eyes sparkled and his face brightened as he described her. When Richard saw the expression on his son's face, he realised that he must have found his true love. Just as he had years ago.

"I'd love to meet this sweet girl."

"She wants to meet you as well."

Everything was fine in Bard's life except for Maidie's absence and the longing he felt for her. His days were monotonous as he toiled between home, school and the restaurant. His only social life these days consisted of writing letters to Maidie and reading those that he received from her. The plans they made together motivated him and helped him stay focused. The days they were going to spend together were going to be the wildest, the most memorable and the most magical time of their lives; they were going to have so many stories to tell their children in the future.

It was March. Bard was sitting down with his books he spread on the coffee table in the living room, sometimes working and sometimes daydreaming. It was freezing cold outside. Even though the winter was coming to an end, the frost and ice did not seem to be ceasing anytime soon. It had been snowing non-stop since last night. It was almost noon, but the sky was dark like it was evening. The gloomy weather slowly drew Bard in as well; he was unusually restless. He got up to brew some tea. Thinking that watching the snowfall might ease his soul, he took his cup and stood by the window, albeit to no avail; his restlessness grew instead. This feeling was not foreign to him, and that disturbed him even more. There it was again; there was no escaping it. The voice from deep within repeated the sentence, "Sing my song." What should he be thinking? What should he be feeling? Someone must have been in trouble again. Should he be feeling afraid? Or was he going to be able to prevent it?

Was that why the fairy was here? It was not easy to endure the confusion and the unknown.

He put on his coat and boots, rushed out, and immersed himself in the freshness of the cold air. The noise in his head got quieter as he focused all his attention on his steps, trying not to slip and fall. The snow was almost up to twenty centimetres deep and the ground was partly frozen. When he walked all the way to the restaurant, Sean was inside, talking with his dad impassionedly. Hurriedly, he started explaining to Bard, as soon as he saw him coming in.

"Did you hear about the accident? The bus to Craignure drifted on the icy road and tumbled down a cliff."

Bard held on to the chair beside him; his head was spinning wildly, his stomach turned, all his limbs went numb and he couldn't do anything but collapse right where he was standing. Sean and his dad took his arms, held him up and seated him on the chair. Though he was apprehensive himself, Cedric managed to instruct Sean, who was looking absolutely worried, "Go get a wet towel, quick." He held Bard's face in his hands. "Are you okay, son?"

The voices seemed to be coming from far away. As he opened his eyes, he saw everything moving in slow motion; all the cells of his body felt as if they were freed from the pull of gravity and he was floating weightlessly. Cedric asked Sean to place the wet towel on his forehead, then ran towards the kitchen.

When Bard came to, he was met with a pair of eyes laden with worry. He leaned forward and shifted his weight on his legs, rubbed his eyes and tried to get up, embarrassed as he saw his own vomit on the floor. "Sorry," he murmured, as Cedric stopped him from getting up, pressing down from his shoulders.

"Sit down now, gather yourself for a second."

After the blood came back to his cheeks, Bard talked, unable to look Sean in the eye. "It was freezing outside. I think I caught a cold."

As Cedric handed him honey and lemon tea, his voice was full of compassion. "Everyone is getting sick these days. Drink this up, it should make you feel better."

When Cedric went to the kitchen and left the two of them alone, Bard looked desperately at his friend. "Were there any deaths?"

Sean had already predicted the reason for his plight and understood that the fairy was at work. He answered in a hoarse voice, hanging his head. "Unfortunately, no one survived…"

Bard cowered with his hands on his face; his voice was barely audible. "I'm so scared, Sean. All of these incidents… I feel like the fairy is getting more and more vicious."

After Bard was done with his tea, the two friends walked back home together. The stillness of nature accompanied their silence and sorrow; all was completely silent. They were surrounded by a deep quiet.

When it was time to translate this sorrow into music, Bard complied with his duty, using his guitar. Once again, it was a divine work of art with a profound emotional intensity. However, the heaviness of his heart lingered and increased; sadness slowly took over his whole being. He was exhausted and felt like he was falling into a dark well as he thought, *Though they are beautiful, I no longer want these melodies, these songs from the fairy; I can't endure another disaster,* just before he fell asleep.

Chapter 14

Spring had arrived and nature was in revival. The trees were under their blanket of green again. All living things were in a hurry. It was a rush to regenerate, propagate and proliferate. It was as the tightly shut gates of life in the winter were wide open now, letting out all its energy. Plants were competing to flourish as fast as possible; the birds were bustling to build their nests and set up a home for soon-to-be-born nestlings, while those who still hadn't got a mate were seeking for a partner with various melodic serenades. All this movement of nature generated a magnificent vigour and ensured the continuation of the cycle of life.

Bard loved to jump on his bike and go into the forest to witness nature's rebirth. Whenever he was tired of working hard or felt troubled, he went to get some fresh air in the forest. He would feel refreshed by the vivacious spark of spring and would feel his creative potential amplify.

Winter had been quite rough. Bard had never before experienced such cold weather and heavy snowfall. The sun hadn't appeared for days on end. Thus, spring glowed with an even brighter light this year. The spring also meant the summer was at the door, which only increased the appeal of the season in Bard's eyes.

Bard was on his usual venture into the forest which had become a routine after-school activity for him. He sat down with his back on the large trunk of the trees, through the leaves of which sunshine gently filtered; he closed his eyes and let the balmy sunrays calm him down and warm his body and soul. The songs of birds permeated the whole forest. As he was listening to the harmony of the forest, suddenly, the thought of the fairy sprang to his mind. He hadn't heard its whisper since the accident and he didn't wish to. What had happened that day bothered him greatly. The fact that he could sense yet do nothing to prevent the terrible accident, just when he was thinking that this gift might be benevolent, shook his faith completely and made him concede that it was utterly useless. Drawing in a deep breath, he opened his eyes slightly, absorbing the blueness of the sky beyond the green leaves. With the thought, *The melody of nature is good enough for me*, he cast the fairy from his mind and tried to focus on the rhythm of the moment.

Spring was over quickly with the busy pace of working at the restaurant and studying for the final exams. His exam results did not come as a surprise. Almost all his grades were As and with these results he was going to be able to get a scholarship at the university he wanted to attend. It was the last weekend before schools closed. He was about to leave home for his graduation ceremony and Richard was fixing his son's tie.

"You are talented and successful. I'm proud of you. You deserve the best. I wish I could offer you a better, more comfortable life."

"Thank you. I know you're trying to do your best, Dad."

"Come on, we're running late," Richard said with teary eyes, patting his shoulder.

All the students were at the ceremony hall, elegantly dressed. Bard looked dashing in his navy-blue suit. It was his father's graduation gift for him.

Students received their diplomas with the cheers and applause of the audience. As they walked upon the stage, they all glimmered with the pride of being one step closer to adulthood and the confidence of successfully finishing a chapter of their lives. As he proudly watched his son on stage, Richard was silently talking to Angela, murmuring, "I wish you could be here to see our son graduate, my love." In that moment, Bard was also thinking of his mother, though with a different perspective. He believed that Angela was watching over him right now, smiling happily and lovingly. Looking up to the sky, he muttered, "Your soul is with us, I can feel it."

After the ceremony, the young students headed towards the beach in groups for an after party. Some people had already made preparations, collecting some wood and twigs for the fire. Another group had arranged drinks; of course, there was alcohol. Throughout the night, they drank and danced around the large bonfire and had a blast. Everyone was having a good time except Bard. The fairy was there again, repeating the same whispers endlessly: "Sing my song." Bard tried not to hear the fairy's call, scared that it was a bad omen. He tried to ignore it to no avail. No matter how much he tried to turn a deaf ear; he was not able to repress the whispers in his mind. He was being pulled closer and closer to the inevitable end.

One of the girls was hastily looking high and low, searching for her friend who had just been sitting on the pier with her. No one had seen her friend; a small search party did a quick look around the place but found no trace. When the question, "She was very drunk, could she have fallen into the sea?" was uttered, it caused everyone to panic. Several of the men, including Sean and Bard, jumped right into the water. Bard was looking around as he silently spoke with the fairy: *I hope you're here to help.* As he swam with frenzied strokes in the dark water, he was startled as his foot touched something. When he dove under the water, he saw her. She was floating still in the void, arms outstretched. He grabbed on to her clothes and yanked her up with all his might, but her body was heavy as lead; he shouted for help. When they dragged her to the beach, they made her spew out the water she had swallowed and gave her mouth-to-mouth resuscitation. There was a hectic turmoil. The girls were kicking and stamping in shrieks and the boys screaming frantically for help. Unfortunately, despite all their efforts, they could not save their friend. By the time the medics arrived at the scene, a bright young light who had just started to shine had gone out.

When Bard got back home, heartbroken and deep in thought, he locked himself in his room. He was utterly devastated. How deeply he wished to believe that the fairy was helping him. The suspicion spreading in his soul since the bus accident in winter was succumbing to hopelessness today. Was it the fairy's duty to hint at the future misfortunes through her songs?

He was grumbling to himself, "To hell with this gift!" As the tears flowed down his cheeks, he picked up his notebook and hurled it out of the window in fury. "Get your melodies and get out of my life!"

Chapter 15

B ARD WAS SHIFTING IN BED, TUCKING HIS HEAD UNDER
the pillow, taking it out, tossing and turning, unable to fall asleep.
Tomorrow was the big day: Maidie was going to come to Tobermory.
As he saw her naive beauty, her sweet smile and her big almond eyes
in his mind's eye, he grew restless with the intensity of longing and the
anticipation of having her back.

Early in the morning he took a shower and got dressed. Richard
was watching his son's hectic state with a grin. "Isn't it too early?"

Bard pressed his lips together, not bothered that his excitement
was clearly visible as he responded with a shrug. "I can't wait. I'll hang
out with Sean for a while, then I'll go to Craignure to meet her."

Bard took the bus to the harbour and saw the ferry approaching
when he got there. As the ferry drew nearer, his heart pumped louder
and louder, his heartbeats almost audible from the outside, like those
of a scared little bird. The moment he saw her, he felt fireworks going
off in all the particles of his body. When the ship was fully docked,
Maidie jumped off the deck and ran straight into Bard's arms. While
in a tight embrace, Bard lifted her feet off the ground and spun her
around. Their passionate reunion and joy infected all those around
them and put a smile on their faces.

When Mr and Mrs McPearson came around, they all got in the
car and the youngsters settled in the backseat. Maidie was sneering
and rolling her eyes, annoyed by her parents' ceaseless enquiries
towards Bard throughout the journey. Both of her parents quite liked
Bard and approved of him as their daughter's boyfriend actually; still,

it wasn't going to stop them from questioning him now that they had the opportunity.

A summer full of hope was at dawn; they could feel that it would come to pass like a reverie.

Every day was more fun and enjoyable than the previous one. At times they went on trips on their bicycles and sometimes they stayed home having long conversations. They were still exploring and getting to know each other mentally and physically; with the vigour of their love and their youth, they savoured carnal sensations with every opportunity they got. The only thing that overshadowed Bard's happiness was his trouble in his mind: *What if the fairy whispers again…?*

In the hilly terrain just outside of town, Maidie was unpacking the picnic basket with Sean's girlfriend Cordelia, while Bard and Sean were collecting brushwood for the fire. After the boys came back and lit the fire, they sat around and ate the sausages they had cooked. After they'd eaten their fill, they started playing charades. They laughed so much that Maidie had to stop the bunch by saying, "That's enough, I'm splitting my sides." They had deliberately chosen this day for camping since there was going to be a meteor shower this midnight. When it was time, they put out the fire and the couples retreated to seclusion away from each other. As they watched the night sky in complete darkness, they were all utterly bewitched. The stars seemed to be within their grasp.

Bard spoke with his eyes fixated on the sky as if he was hypnotised. "Our world is tiny in this vast eternity and we are smaller than a speck of dust. We are part of an extraordinary, mysterious system. I get scared thinking about it sometimes."

Maidie's gaze was full of determination. "It doesn't scare me at all. The system works as it should, all that we experience are things that are bound to happen. It may feel right or wrong for us at the time, but when we look from a bigger perspective, everything flows like the rivers finding the sea." After a deep inhale, she slightly nudged Bard. "Enough philosophising. Let's make a wish for every shooting star."

A while later, Maidie clapped her hands cheerfully, looking at Bard with her big bright eyes. "How lucky we are! All our wishes will come true." Their eyes met, their bodies slowly drew closer and when their lips touched, the sky blessed them with its magnificent spectacle. They felt as if they were in a fairy tale. The fireworks were lighting up the dark night when they became one. This was the most intense and the most beautiful experience they ever had. For a while they just dozed in a cosy embrace.

With the effect of their heavenly experience and the enchantment of the night, Bard decided to tell her all about the whispers of the fairy from the very beginning. Cedric, his father, the bus accident and what had happened on graduation night... How he hurled his notebook out that night in desolation and despair, how his father found the notebook on the street and brought it back in the morning...

Maidie was mystified. "Why didn't you tell me before?"

"I was embarrassed, I thought you would find it stupid."

Maidie's gaze deepened; pride shone in her eyes. "When I first saw you, I knew you were someone special. Your emotions, insights and intuitions are strong." She reached out and grabbed his cheek. "I love you, Bard McLoyd."

"I love you too."

As their gaze intensified and their lips met once more, they felt hungry for each other like the earth longing for rain after a long drought.

⁓

When Bard introduced Maidie to his father, they both liked each other very much. Whenever she came around, Richard's face lit up and he was all smiles. Even Bard was surprised at their easy-going conversations. "You are not as talkative with me, I'm getting jealous," he would say. For him, it was a joy that the two got along so well. He felt like this was what had been missing in their home, 'the spirit of a woman'. For the first time since they'd lost Angela, this place did not only feel like a shelter for them, but like a 'warm home'. As the air filled with jokes and laughter, Bard's delight soared, and his admiration and love for Maidie multiplied. He prayed incessantly that he would never hear the voice of the fairy again, which would be the only thing that would ruffle his temper.

Occasionally, they helped Maidie's father Ewin with his research. Maidie's heart was full of love for animals and nature; she could observe them for hours without getting bored. It was a real pleasure to research and learn about them. That was why she wanted to pursue veterinary medicine as a career. For her, this was not just work; she truly enjoyed it. The same was true for Bard and music. Music was his whole world. For him, it was the best and easiest way to express himself. Hence, both of them were lucky to be pursuing their passions professionally.

Summer flew by in the blink of an eye, busy in flurry, fun and explorations. On the one hand, they were sad that these joyful and carefree days were soon coming to an end; on the other hand, they were excited about their new life at the university. They only had three weeks left. Maidie was going to go back home with her family in a few days, make her preparations, then travel to Glasgow to meet with Bard at the start of the semester.

Everything was fine; however, there was a gnawing worry in Bard's soul for no reason. To be fair, it was not completely without reason. For a few nights now, he had been dreaming of the fairy, but it disappeared before he could talk to her. He would agonise over hearing the whispers again whenever he remembered his dream. He did not want to bother Maidie by telling her about his troubles, but he couldn't keep it to himself any longer. He told Sean about his situation, who was the only person he could confide in and his closest friend.

Though he tried not to show Bard, Sean was in fact worried for his friend. These strange intuitions of his friend were starting to scare him. But now, he needed to be supportive. He put his hands in his pockets and shrugged, trying to act unbothered. "You've been very stressed lately. You are leaving home for the first time. I suppose starting a new life would be as scary as it would be exciting. Also, if I know you well, which I'm sure I do, you are worried, wondering, *What if I cannot succeed?* All of these must be putting you under a lot of strain."

He continued, stroking Bard's back lightly, "Is there anything you wanted to and couldn't achieve? Besides, you are not alone – Maidie is with you and you will be supporting each other. A beautiful future awaits you. Just focus on the good things and try to calm down, okay?

Forget about the fairy whispers. You have a real fairy next to you, Maidie. You'll soon leave this place and the fairy all behind anyway."

Bard's tensed shoulders relaxed; the timid look in his eyes was replaced with a glow of excitement. He threw his arm around Sean's shoulder. "You are the best and only friend I have ever had. If only you were coming with me – that would be the best."

Sean was not going to attend university but instead was going to work with his father at the family restaurant. This place had been owned by the O'Canons for three generations. Sean was their only child, which meant that if he left, it would be the end of the family business. Sean would never want that to happen. He had no other career goals anyway; he was quite content here. Moreover, his relationship with Cordelia was going great and he didn't wish to lose it.

"I'll see you when you come over for holidays and I will visit you frequently as well. You did promise to take me to some fun parties, don't forget!"

His friend's kind efforts relieved Bard a little, though that mixture of worry and fear was still haunting him.

Chapter 16

I T WAS MAIDIE'S LAST DAYS BEFORE LEAVING TOBERMORY.
They rode their bikes to the beach that they loved so much, with
its white sandy shore extending as far as the eyes could see. The wind
was strong, the atmosphere was airy and fresh, besprinkled with the
specks dispersing off the vigorous waves. For a long while, they just
enjoyed the fresh air and the view, locked in an embrace. Interrupting
the silence, Maidie freed herself from Bard's arms and turned to face
him, crossing her legs, then reaching out and holding his hand. Her
large amber eyes sparkled with hope on her delicate little face.

"Let's talk about the good days to come."

It was just like her: always enjoying the moment, looking at things
on the bright side and focusing on the good with her positive point
of view. She had realised Bard's distress and wanted to provide some
respite. She put her hand on his cheek, her gaze full of wisdom.

"Life is too short to waste our time with bad thoughts, worries,
fears and regrets – let's appreciate and enjoy this beautiful moment
we have."

Without taking her eyes off Bard's, she reached for his lips, then
paused briefly and: "Do we have a deal?" she said, waiting.

"Deal," Bard whispered, eagerly responding to the pull of her sweet
lips… They sat there for another hour and contemplated their new life
with hope and glee. They both couldn't wait for it any longer.

When it was time to return, they got on their bikes and set off. As
they rode, laughing and joking around, Bard suddenly heard its voice.
The fairy was whispering again, and the whispers were getting louder

117

and louder, capturing his whole being. He began to feel dizzy and out of breath. He pulled his bike to the curbside to recover, trying to catch his breath. *What's going on? Where did this come from all of a sudden? I don't want to hear your voice.* Overwhelmed with chaotic fear, he did not realise that Maidie had already rode too far away from him. He should have kept her close. He started pedalling again at breakneck speed. They were going downhill on a winding road; it was difficult to catch up. He called out her name, asking her to slow down. "Maidie!" The wind sent back an echo of his voice; he shouted even more. "Maidie! Slow down, I can't keep up." As Maidie looked back to see what he was yelling for, she could not catch the sight of the vehicle turning the corner. At that instant, as if watching a slow-motion movie, Bard saw Maidie fly across the air with the impact of collision, then hit hard on the ground. "No, no!" He was screaming at the top of his chest. "No, please God, please…" He hurled his bike and ran to her side. The way her body was positioned on the floor did not look good at all. As Bard frantically shouted her name, he felt as if he was going to rip away the veins in his throat. His tears were a roaring river sweeping whatever else came out of his mouth and his nose. Maidie parted the large hazel eyes that Bard could never get tired of seeing and closed them once again after she said, "My love," with a faint voice. A single drop of tear was let loose from her eyes as they shut, travelling from her temple and falling into Bard's hand, just under her head.

He wasn't sure when exactly the ambulance arrived or how they got to the hospital. As he sat there in the waiting room with his hands covered his face, numb and insensate, Bard could only hear the sorrowful music of the fairy echoing within him, eating away at his brain. A violent tremor took over his whole being when he opened his eyes and saw Maidie's parents talking with the doctor only to be left keeled over, drowning in sobs. The rest was an endless blackness…

Bard's life turned upside down in seconds; he disconnected from the world. How could such a thing happen? She was so young. She was lively and full of energy. The coldness of death did not suit her. They had a lot of things to do, a future to look forward to. What was going to happen now? How was he going to be able to go on without her? He wished to remain forever in the pit of the darkness that he was in now, never to come out. He did not know for how many minutes or hours he stayed in that doubled-over position, nor did he want to learn. Was someone talking to him or was he hearing strange voices? At some point, he thought he saw his father's glassy eyes staring at him.

When he regained consciousness, he was lying in his room at home. With the bitter realisation that all that had happened was not a nightmare, his tears began to stream unceasingly. He cried with the thought, *It should have been me instead of her. I should have died instead.* He cried for the dying out of her bright light full of love, for his own life lightless and dark, for life's cruelty and for despair... The sense of guilt was burning through his heart, corroding his insides.

If only... If only he hadn't heard the voice of the fairy; if only he hadn't been distraught and shouted at her, she might be alive now. He pulled the duvet over his head, curled up in a foetal position under it, repeating to himself, "What have I done?" He grew hollower and dried with his pain flowing out in tears; anger filled its place. "Damn you, fairy, I do not want you. Leave me alone, I don't want you or your music, get out of my soul or out from wherever you are..."

Richard and Sean could not find the words to comfort him. What could anyone say in such a situation? What words, what sentences could ever lessen this grief? They did the only thing they could do and stood by him, shared his sorrow as he lived through his pain.

Maidie's funeral was held three days after the accident. Bard went to Edinburgh to attend the ceremony with Sean. They didn't speak a word along the way, unless absolutely necessary. They arrived in the evening and settled in a small hostel. After a little rest, they visited the church that the ceremony would be held in and prayed. When they left the church, Sean insisted that they grabbed something to eat. Bard went to bed as soon as they got back to the hostel and fell asleep immediately as if he was tranquilised. Though sleep was no different than being awake. His emotions were benumbed; he didn't feel a thing, not even in the slightest. Everything was devoid of colour now; the pitch-black nothingness was everywhere. He himself had died with Maidie; the only difference was that his body remained in the physical world.

When Bard took out the navy-blue suit he brought for the ceremony, he collapsed on the bed, shaken by the vision that came to life in his memory. Maidie had been rummaging around his closet one evening, as they were hanging out in his room. She put her hand on the suit, and with a flutter of her eyelashes: "I want to see in the suit you wore for graduation, put it on for me."

"Now?"

Maidie eagerly nodded yes.

"Well, I'll be damned," Bard said; she watched him with affection as he dressed.

When he lastly put on his jacket, Maidie took him in from head to toe. "Wow! Who are you? I want to leave my boyfriend and start dating you, you handsome thing." She grabbed the collar of his shirt and pulled him towards her, kissing him feverishly.

As Bard unwittingly caressed the collar of the jacket where her fingers had once touched, teardrops soaked the fabric. Sean put his hand on his friend's shoulder and gave him a squeeze. They looked at each other for a brief, silent moment. They had to get going now.

Bard had brought his guitar all the way here; it was on his shoulder now, as they made their way to church. Sean was wondering why but didn't ask.

Although it was quite crowded in the church, there was still a deep silence. The Maidie's coffin was right there in front of him; it was decorated with wildflowers. There was a photograph of her gazing out at them with her usual loving and warm smile. Mr and Mrs McPearson sat in the front row, hand in hand, stooping in pain. When the couple noticed Bard approaching and caressing the coffin; they got up to hug him, then seated him next to them. The priest gave his sermon and they recited prayers; there was not a single person who could hold back their tears as they sang hymns together. Her aunt and her teacher stepped on the pulpit and gave speeches sharing their memories of her. After the ceremony, they went to the cemetery. As they waited for everyone to gather, Bard talked with Ewin and the priest. After they recited their prayers and lowered the coffin into the pit with the priest's prompt, Bard stepped forward with his guitar and played the song he'd composed for Maidie in tears. When he was finished, he kissed his guitar and put it next to the coffin. His shoulders were drooped down low; his legs were barely able to carry his weight. He whispered quietly, with his last drop of power remaining, "A part of me will always be there with you. I'll never ever forget you. Rest now my angel, until we meet again."

When they returned to Tobermory, Richard gingerly enquired about the ceremony and how the family was. He thought maybe it would be good for him to open up. But for Bard, this was equal to torture. He wanted to take refuge in the silence of his room and never leave it. He lay down on his bed, stared at the ceiling and lay there for a while. He didn't know how much time had passed when there was a knock on his door, it was Sean. Cedric had sent food and beer from the restaurant. Only the sounds of cutlery could be heard as they sat down and ate their meal together. After dinner, Richard retreated to his room and left the two boys alone. *Maybe he'll talk to his friend. He'll pour out his grief,* he hoped.

Sean tried to start a conversation once or twice, but it was as if he was speaking to a wall; his words hung unclaimed in the air. *He needs time,* Sean reckoned. *He may never forget, but his pain will lessen with time.* As he was pondering about this, Bard went into his room and came back with a file in his hand. He was glaring with fury; his brows furrowed. With a firm and sharp determination, he threw the file in front of Sean.

"Take this, Sean. I don't want to see it again. You can do whatever you want with it, just keep it away from me!"

Sean knew what was in the file without even opening it. These must be those magnificent songs and melodies Bard had created; his greatest love after Maidie, his purpose in life.

Bard blamed himself fervently for Maidie's death. For him, this was the only punishment fitting, to sacrifice the most precious part of him, the thing that made him cling to life despite everything, the thing that made him who he is.

Chapter 17

Tobermory, 2016

As the sun was setting, the ruby red of the sky was gradually turning into a purple haze and the weak rays of sun gently seeping through the windows were slowly and unwillingly pulling back. When Sean was done speaking, Melissa's heart was smouldering like the flames of the fireplace that she was mindlessly staring at, while her soul shivered with a coldness like that of the freezing winds of the Arctic. Her tears poured for her father's broken and young heart, his losses and the twinge of his conscience. She always guessed that her father had some qualms about his past, but what she had heard had exceeded her suppositions. Now, she could understand better why his heart was so weak, as to not be able to survive the first big heart attack he'd had at the age of sixty-five.

With the feel of the blanket that William was putting on her, Melissa once again returned to her senses. She clung closely to the blanket as Sean put his hand on her shoulder; his voice was full of compassion. "You can go upstairs to rest a little, if you wish to."

Melissa grabbed the hand on her shoulder and looked at her father's bosom friend gratefully. "No, I feel comfortable here, I just need a little time."

William spoke with a tender voice. "Okay, but call out if you need anything, we will be in the kitchen."

As they were just getting out of the door, Melissa called after them. "Sean!"

When the man turned to her, he saw Melissa looking like a little girl with her eyes swollen and her nose bright red from crying.

"Thank you. I cannot possibly put into words what today meant for me."

On the sofa, tucked under her blanket, Melissa was trying to give meaning to all that she'd heard. With her eyes closed, she envisaged her father's childhood and the early years of his youth; she felt the agony he must have felt in the depths of her heart, the agony of losing the two most important women in his life. Why had he punished himself so severely and tormented his innocent, loving soul. *Oh, Daddy, what have you done to yourself? Why did you carry such a heavy burden on your shoulders for years? Don't you have any pity for yourself?* She moaned inside. There was also the fairy – what should she be thinking about that? Could it be real? Or was it only an image of his wounded soul? The chances were that her father was suffering from some psychological difficulties due to a grave trauma. It was hard to believe that her father, a reasonable man whom she knew to be of sound mind, had gone through such tribulations. Now, that it was all falling into place, she could see the reasoning behind his contempt of music. If only he had shared it with them, maybe they could have helped him remedy his wounds. Alas, he had buried it all so deep in his soul that even he had forgotten the existence of his hurt.

Melissa felt tired and even worn out with the weight of what she had learned. She must have had dozed off for a while since she was startled awake by a sudden clatter coming from inside. She looked around, confounded; it took some time for her to remember where she was. William's spry voice arouse from inside. Then, the voices turned into whispers. She felt the need to pull herself together; she sat up, straightened herself and took a deep breath. She then got up and folded the blanket, put it back on the sofa, and went to the kitchen to join the O'Canons.

All of them were busy at work. Melissa watched them; her sorry eyes filled with guilt. "I'm very sorry, I'm causing you so much trouble. Please at least let me help you."

Cordelia gave her a warm, motherly smile. "Don't worry, honey, Will is here helping us anyway." She nudged William with her elbow.

Melissa turned to him this time and asked again, "Let me help you then, please, or I'll feel bad."

William flashed a mischievous grin like that of naughty children. "Well, I never refuse an offer of help." Despite her tangled and wearying emotional state, she couldn't help but think how sweet the dimples revealed by his sincere smile were.

They set the table together. At dinner, they eased off with the wine William brought as they enjoyed the meat sauté prepared by Cordelia. Sean gave some information on Tobermory and the Isle of Mull comprising it. William told some funny stories about the customers who'd had a bit too much to drink in the pub. Feeling warm and comforted, Melissa was slightly heartened after the merry, mellow and wholehearted evening together; however, she still got lost in thought from time to time.

At the end of the night, when it was time to return to the hotel, Cordelia regarded her anxiously. "Stay with us, at least for tonight."

Sean was also worried. He threw his arm over Cordelia's shoulder. "Yes, yes, Cordelia is right. This had been quite a shock for you, we will be worried with you all alone."

Melissa's cheeks flushed red; as she gazed at each of them gratefully her shoulders loosened with the ease of surrender. "You are too kind."

William quickly stood up and put on his jacket. "All right then, you are staying; and since that subject is over with, I'll go now. If you want, I can show you around tomorrow."

Melissa's eyes sparkled. "I would love that. But you may have things to do, I wouldn't want to get in the way."

As William's lips curled into a smile, his lovely dimples appeared once again. "Wending my way in nature is a part of my job. I'd go even if you wouldn't want to join."

"How do you mean? I thought you ran a pub?"

"Well, I'll keep you wondering until tomorrow, I'll tell you when we meet. Is nine in the morning good?"

"Good, I'll see you in the morning then."

After William's departure, Cordelia walked her up the stairs, saying, "Come on, honey, let me show you your room."

Melissa turned to Sean; she felt closer to her father when she was next to him and she was grateful for the feeling. She reached out and kissed his cheek softly. "Being with you, hearing what you had to share… I cannot possibly tell you how much it means to me. Thank you so much for everything, good night."

Melissa removed her clothes in the small room which could only hold a bed and dresser, then hung them behind the door, going to bed in her underwear. Her head was pounding from exhaustion. Thoughts, visions and voices floated in her mind uncontrollably. When she realised that she had not yet spoken to her mother, albeit hesitantly, she decided not to call. She herself was yet to be able to take in all that she had heard now, so how was she going to tell her mother about it all? As she was finally able to fall asleep, she had to battle with the mysterious dreams about her father once again.

William oozed with positive energy when he arrived at exactly nine o'clock in the morning; squeezing his mother Cordelia's cheeks and kissing her, he chirped, "Good morning, everybody!"

Melissa looked at her watch as she nodded. "You live up to your reputation for being punctual."

Cordelia gestured at the breakfast table that she was just clearing. "Are you hungry? Sit down and eat something."

"No, I'm not hungry, but I'll have a bite of your delicious strawberry jam." He put some jam on a small piece of bread and gulped it down.

Melissa had the feeling that he had just taken a bite to please her; she really enjoyed the warm, affectionate communication between the mother and son. William loved appeasing others; she had experienced it first-hand many times since they'd met. Inevitably, she was reminded of Ron. For him, his own happiness and comfort came first at all times; only after that, Ron would ever consider others' contentment. How different they were from each other.

Sean took a sip of his steaming-hot tea and placed it back on the table. "Did you include Staffa in your travel plans?"

"Unfortunately, no. There won't be enough time for that today. I thought we could spare another day for it. We need to arrange a boat beforehand as well."

He looked at Melissa with a questioning gaze.

"Ahh! Of course, that'll be okay," Melissa replied. She wasn't sure if she was ready to go right to that place where it had all started and face everything, but she knew that she had to get to the root of her problems sooner or later to be able to move forward. She had to push through; she had to find the answers for the questions in her mind to finally be at peace.

"Come on then, let's get going if you're ready."

William opened the door for Melissa and waited for her to get into the car; he then got in himself, started the engine and, throwing her a loving glance, asked, "Are you ready to explore your father's country?"

"I haven't been readier and more eager to do anything in a long time."

Melissa surveyed her surroundings, trying not to miss anything, until they drove out of town, then turned her attention to William. "Alright, I'm listening. You were going to tell me about what you do for work?"

"I work as a volunteer at the wildlife conservation foundation."

"Wow! That is great. I have always wanted to take part in something like that. I never had the opportunity unfortunately, because of my busy schedule."

"Here is your opportunity. First, we will go around and check if everything is okay, then we will visit the foundation's clinic to see if they need anything, or if they need any help; would you like that?"

Melissa's face brightened as her eyes glimmered with flickers of admiration. "Excellent."

For about three hours they drove around and observed various parts of the island, usually near the seaside or the riverbeds. They had to get out of the car in some places and go on foot. When Melissa slid over the moss-covered rocks as they walked along the stream, William swiftly caught her and kept her from falling. He took her hand and brought her to a safer area. At that instance they were both startled by the unexpected pitter-patter of their hearts.

Melissa was thoroughly enchanted by the untouched nature around her. Being present at the existence of such unspoiled habitats had touched a hidden part in her soul, making her aware of those wishes that she never knew existed. "How wonderful would it be to live here!" She recalled the parks they had walked in with her father. The image of his peaceful expression as he walked among the trees appeared before her eyes; her heart ached. Perhaps, her father was trying to satisfy his longing for such green places, or perhaps he was imagining himself back in those places where he had been born and raised.

Melissa pulled away from her thoughts with the car coming to a stop and gazed in astonishment at the old, decrepit building they were parked in front of. "Is this the clinic?"

William gave her a sorry look as he got out of the car. "Sadly, the foundation hasn't got much income left. It hasn't been able to afford the repairs."

They greeted the secretary at the desk as they entered. There wasn't any furniture except for a few chairs; the paint was bubbling on the walls due to humidity. As Melissa looked around, her heart sinking, a chubby woman in her late forties, with a brown, round face, walked down the corridor. "William, hello."

"Hello, Lucy, let me introduce you to our guest Melissa from America."

Lucy held out her hand for a shake. "Nice to meet you, welcome."

Melissa smiled sincerely as she gripped her outstretched hand. Her eyes roamed around the room once again. "You are working under tough conditions here."

William interrupted. "Melissa is also a veterinarian."

"Oh, is that so! That means we are colleagues then."

"Yes. But I have always dealt with domestic animals, cats and dogs; I haven't got much experience with wild animals."

Lucy motioned her hand as if to say, 'let's go'. "Then follow me, I'll introduce you to some friends. I think they might pique your interest." She opened the door at the end of the hallway. "This is the post-treatment care room." She stood beside a cage with a white-tailed eagle in it and looked at it lovingly. "This friend has hurt its wing. When it was found, it was wandering about and waiting to be someone's prey."

Melissa marvelled at the animal. "How shiny its feathers are, and what a noble bearing it has."

Meanwhile, Lucy had approached another cage. She pointed at the fawn lying on the ground with one foot plastered, looking around with doleful eyes. "This cute little one you see here owes its life to Will."

Melissa grabbed a pinch of grass and fed the baby with one hand, as she softly caressed it with the other. She glanced enquiringly at Will.

"The expedition we did today was to locate animals in such situations."

While they continued their conversation in the seats with frayed covers in Lucy's small room, they were unaware that the baby deer they had just seen was now able to step on its strained foot easily. Two colleagues exchanged information about the equipment they used. The equipment in the clinic, like all the other things, was old, but they were enough. Lucy had a sorrowful expression as she said, "These are my last days here, I'm quitting soon."

"Ah! I am very sorry."

"It's not only me. All other employees have not been paid for months as well. We all have families to take care of."

"You must have talked to the authorities. What are they saying about this situation?"

William explained, "The foundation was established forty years ago. At that time, the university was funding it."

"What about now?"

"The founder had spent all his wealth on this place; while he was still alive, he did everything to keep this place afloat. He was a lecturer at the university, but when he passed away, no one burdened themselves to care about the place, so it was neglected."

"It such a shame that a charitable place like this, founded by such care and love, is left to ruin."

Lucy sighed. "It's just a matter of time for it to close down for good."

Melissa was moved by what she had heard and saw. "I wish there was something I could do. If you'd agree, I'll happily come up here to help while I'm staying here."

"I'd be glad. Our door is always open to you, whenever you are free."

As they got into the car, William asked, "How about dinner? Are you hungry?"

Melissa smiled. "I thought you would never ask."

This little trip did Melissa good; it eased the shock of what she had learned the day before. All through the trip, she had seen everything around her through her father's eyes and felt the peace of being with him within her soul.

When they arrived at the pub, they sat down and talked about the trip as they nibbled on their seafood salads. William wanted to enquire about Melissa's feelings concerning what she had learned about her father as they sipped their coffees after dinner, but he was afraid to ask. Similarly, Melissa was silent as she worried about bothering him with her problems ...

Melissa reflected on how easy it was to talk with William as she walked to her hotel. He was considerate; he really listened to the person he was speaking with and cared about their opinions. With these thoughts, her longing for her father emerged once again. As she looked over at the streets she was passing through, she noted that she was yet to see the house where her father lived as a child and reminded herself to ask Sean whether he could take her there.

When she got to her room, she called her mother first. She told Judith about Sean, Cordelia and about her trip with William.

"Hmm! That boy William sounds like a good one." Judith jokingly sounded her daughter out.

"Mum! You are meddling even across the ocean," Melissa complained in jest.

They laughed and chatted causally. Melissa shared only a small, inconsequential part of what she learned about her father's past. She didn't want to cause her pain. It was best to tell her everything face to face when she got back.

Melissa's sleep was interrupted by waking dreams throughout the night. Her father was in all of them. In some, he disappeared in a fog; in others, he spoke, repeating the same sentence: "You have a special power." She had gotten used to these dreams ever since she arrived at Tobermory.

She walked straight to the clinic after breakfast. Lucy was both surprised and happy to see her. The fact that there were still such selfless people around somewhat dulled her desperation.

"Heyy! Welcome."

Melissa gave a cheery shrug. "I have no plans for today – I thought I may be useful here."

Lucy gathered the thin auburn strands of hair falling on her round face and fastened them with a small hair clip. Her eyes were the same colour as the blue sweater she wore over her jeans, and there was an excited glint in her gaze. She turned and glanced at Melissa while hastily putting some supplies in her bag; the lines on her forehead were enough for Melissa to discern her concern.

"You came just in time. One of our volunteers called and told us that they have found a stranded dolphin. We need to get there immediately. There is no time to waste."

They both jumped in the car and quickly made their way to the shore where the dolphin was found. The volunteer who'd given them the information was waiting for them when they arrived. Lucy talked with the man while taking her tool kit out from the boot of the car, whereas Melissa, who had moved nearer, was staring at the creature in awe. "What a wonderful thing you are. What's the matter? What were you doing out of the water?" She ran her hands over its body while she talked to the animal. "Ahh! Here, I think I found the problem – there is a bite mark just near the side of the fin, someone must have hurt you bad." At once, the dolphin began to twist and squirm. Melissa was startled as if she was coming out of a trance.

Lucy knelt beside her. "Okay, little one, now let's send you where you belong." She looked at Melissa gratefully. "Either it was in shock and just calmed down, or you have a magic touch."

The three of them placed a large piece of cloth under the dolphin together with great difficulty, then carried it to a depth where it would be able to swim by itself. And then, the happy ending... The young animal swiftly swam away and met its family waiting for it in the deep blue. Four dolphins hopped out the water several times with synchronised jumps then plunged back into the sea. When they finally disappeared, Melissa's eyes were brimming with tears from the intensity of the emotions evoked by these magical, miraculous moments and the glorious scenes she'd witnessed.

"This is an astounding, marvellous feeling."

Lucy raised an eyebrow. "I thought you would be used to this."

Melissa paused as she was drying her wet legs with the towel. "The difference is that the owners of the pets that come to my clinic just say what their complaints are, and I just piece together the puzzle. Whereas here, you are communicating with the wildlife head-on. Your work is admirable."

"Thank you, but wasn't that exactly what you just did? You talked to that dolphin, you reached out and touched it. It is a wonderful feeling to be able to help living creatures in such ways, no matter whether they are wild or domesticated. Animals have a strong intuition; they can sense kindness and compassion very easily and react accordingly. In truth, us humans have this power as well and our lives would be much easier if only we could use it more."

Lucy's words were true and honest. Realising that 'trusting one's intuitions' was an issue that she came across quite frequently these days, she took it as a sign to hone her abilities in that regard.

When she got back to the hotel and changed out of her wet clothes, Melissa was eager to tell William about her experience. She went straight to the pub without lingering; she was surprised by her own disappointment when she couldn't find him there. She had never before felt this ardent need to share her emotions with anyone other than her mother and father, certainly not with Ron. Since she was already out, she decided to visit Sean. Besides, maybe if she were to catch him while he was free, he would be kind enough to show her to her father's old house.

Sean was sitting behind the counter at the restaurant. When he saw Melissa, his face lit up. He grabbed her arm and led her to a table by the window; they sat opposite each other. He reached out and took Melissa's hands in his palms. "First, tell me if you are hungry, then tell me about all the places you have seen today."

Melissa was chilled to the bone after the incident during the day; she still hadn't warmed up completely. She smiled. "I wouldn't say no to a warm soup."

Sean motioned at the waiter, ordered, then sat back. He wasn't going to talk about the past unless Melissa brought it up herself. "I'm all ears now. Tell me, what is your impression of this place?"

As Melissa spoke earnestly and enthusiastically about her trip with William, the virginal beauty of the nature and what she had gone through today, she did not ask any questions about her father and what she learned about him the other day.

When Sean asked her about Bard's life in America, Melissa ran her eyes over the restaurant and took a deep breath. "You know what, I can tell you that our restaurant there was almost a replica of this one. I think that's a part of the reason why I feel so at home in here."

Sean took Melissa's hands in his own and lightly caressed them. "I'm glad you feel that way." He glanced around then spoke in a sorrowful voice, as if he was talking to himself. "He ended up doing the same thing that I do all the way across the ocean, though what great hopes he had."

Melissa sat up straight; her face fell. "But he was very good at his job. He was successful, he worked with a loving dedication and, most importantly, he was happy."

Sean's cheeks flushed. "Ohh! I think that was ill-phrased. I'm sure he was happy. He had a wife who loved and cherished him, and a sweet daughter like you. I just wanted to make a point about how life is full of surprises and how difficult it is to ever predict what's to become of us."

Melissa regretted her sudden stern reproach. "Sorry, I am yet to come to terms with what I learned about him. I think I may be a little envious of his past," she said as she shifted uneasily. When she started talking once again, her voice was warm with the cosiness of the past memories. "My mother fell in love with my father at first sight, 'I was enthralled by his mysterious, reserved nature,' she would always say. Whereas my father was attracted to her because of her forbearing, loving and trusting disposition. I don't ever remember them arguing. They always listened to each other with understanding and sought a common ground. I was his princess – he used to read the same fairy tales over and over again in my childhood with his sweet, soft voice; and when I grew up, he became my best friend."

Sean's blue beady eyes were gazing under his drooping eyelids with compassion. He was proud of his friend, and he was glad that he found happiness. "Your father was a man with a big heart, he had enough love for everyone. This is a quality of his that would never change; besides, it is obvious that he raised you with love."

Melissa smiled gratefully as a tiny teardrop dropped from the tip of her lash.

Back in her room, Melissa lay down early on the bed to rest; she had what Sean had said on her mind. It was true that life was full of surprises. Sometimes in our journey of life, we will encounter paths and turns that we never expected, and they will change our direction completely. Just like what had happened to her father... Just like how his trauma had taken him and carried him across the ocean... Just like this past year for her and now... The change in her emotions, in her perception of life after the death of her father, this journey and all the different windows opening to dissimilar views of life... They were all surprises from the universe. Who knows how many changes were waiting still in front of her, that she did not know of, that she could not predict...?

She was plucked away from her thoughts by the sound of the phone. It was William calling. "You stopped by today; sorry we couldn't meet. I had travelled to the mainland for work, I just got back. So... How is everything? Did you have a good day?" As he spoke, Melissa realised that his voice made her feel safe and happy.

She hoped that the joy in her voice was not very obvious. "Yes, yes, it was a great day, I had some remarkable experiences." She then gave him a little recap of the day.

"I would have loved to be there with you. How about we go for a walk tomorrow morning?"

"That would be great."

A tinge of relief was sensed from William's voice. "Would half past seven be too early? I usually go for a walk around that time, but if you want to do it later, that's fine too."

Melissa answered hurriedly, "No, please don't mess up your routine for me. I also get up early, it's fine."

After hanging up, Melissa caught the image of herself smiling goofily in the mirror opposite the bed. A question passed through her mind: *What's happening to me?* But she shrugged and said, "I don't want to think about it now," and silenced the enquiries of her inner voice.

⁓

Melissa was awake when the alarm clock went off at seven; she was enjoying the view of the sea and the sunrise while sipping her coffee. William was waiting for her, trying to hold back Foam, when she came out the hotel door just in time.

"Good morning," Melissa said as she crouched down to pet the dog. Foam licked her face excitedly as if to give her a kiss.

"Hey, all this show of love is starting to get on my nerves. What is this infatuation that you two have for each other? It's only been a few days and I've already lost favour," William chided jokingly; upon which Melissa whispered to the dog's ear, "He's just jealous."

The atmosphere was inspiriting, with the smell of fresh dew of the morning mingling with the scent of seaweed carried by the gentle breeze from the sea. They walked in the forest for a while, climbing up a little pathway. Neither the sky above nor the earth below was visible. Dense, dark green vegetation covered everything around them. The gurgling of the small creek seemed to thrill the birds the same way that it did Melissa. When they walked through the forest and arrived at a clearing, she wanted to prance across the green wilderness stretching as far as the eye could see, just like Foam, and frolic with joy. Her freckled cheeks were flushed; her moss-green eyes were sparkling as she looked at William. "I feel great."

William thought she radiated like the sun and felt his heart bundling up in her warmth. "You'll be even more impressed once we get to our destination," he said; a tiny volcano erupted inside Melissa's soul when she saw his dimpled smile. When they finally concluded their climb and reached the top of the hill, the view from the summit really did take her breath away.

The sky and the sea were one; the blue spread through the horizon. Except for a few small islets, the vast ocean extended out endlessly. The waves that resembled little white spots from afar grew larger as they approached the shore, and as they splashed onto the rocks, the scatter of the tiny droplets formed rainbows. Melissa stretched out her arms and inhaled deep breaths. When she uttered, "I sense the eternity and I feel that I am a part of it," without parting her gaze from the sea, William urged, "Now close your eyes." He seized her by her shoulders and turned her around to face the opposite direction. From this point of view, she could see the endless plains blanketed in different shades of green and the misty hills which looked like they had emerged from mystical tales.

Melissa put her hands over her chest just above her heart. When she turned her grateful gaze to William to say, "Thank you so much for sharing such beautiful wonders with me, I think I fell in love with this place," their eyes lingered on each other for a second.

Melissa could strangely feel the presence of her father as William replied, "I'd be happy if I could endear your father's homeland to you." She felt that she and her father had met somewhere within the infinity and they were seeing with same eyes, feeling the same profound peace.

The way back was much less tiring since it was downhill. They laughed along as Foam chased squirrels around and merrily made their way back to town. Once they arrived, William suggested, "We earned a good breakfast, let's get warm croissants from the bakery and go over to the pub."

"Hmm! I love that offer. I'm so hungry that I can already smell the croissants."

The kitchen wasn't big, but it was useful. William took one of the pans hanging over the middle counter and broke two eggs in it, the ease of his movements revealing his experience.

The earnestness that was sparked in Melissa's gaze was also reflected in her voice as she spoke. "Please let me help you. Lately, I've gotten too used to having everything prepared for me. I feel like royalty, I'll have a hard time when I go back home."

As he was slicing tomatoes, William suddenly stopped, as an idea had been sparked in his mind; he put down the knife and leaned against the counter on his hands with a playful squint in his eyes.

"It was said in the legend that the lost princess of the mysterious king would one day return to this land. The legends are true then, it must be you." He was laughing as he pretended to bow to her. He then noticed the clouds of sadness briefly passing through Melissa's eyes. "Sorry, I spoke thoughtlessly."

Standing on the other side of the counter, Melissa noticed how mindful this handsome, lovable man was. "No, on the contrary, it's the first time someone other than my dad has complimented me, telling me I am a princess. It was a compliment, wasn't it?" She chuckled. She had never felt as valued as this during her relationship with Ron. He never noticed the sadness in her gaze, never tried to cheer her up; in short, he didn't make any effort for her. Whereas now, this caring, considerate man really did make her feel cherished.

They were drinking coffee after the breakfast that they had prepared together when Melissa looked over timidly at William. "William, do you mind if I ask a private question?"

"Will," he said, making a welcoming gesture with his hands. "My close friends call me Will."

"Well, Will, did you ever wish to leave here?"

The man's gaze was determined; he was leaning on his arms on the table. "No, I never did. I love being here, in touch with nature. In big cities, people tend to ebb away within all that turmoil. 'A simple and sincere life', that is my motto. Also, here I have all the things I love and everything I am blessed with in life, especially all the people I want to be with, my family, my job…"

Melissa gazed at him with admiration. "You know what, I think you're lucky. Most people either don't know what they want, or they do but it's not within their reach."

"Yes, I am aware of it and thankful for it as well." He took a sip of his coffee, put the cup on the saucer and leaned back. "Still, we do create our own luck a little bit. The choices we made in the past, the places we were in, the people we came across helped us to be what we are in the present, whether we were aware of it or not; and the present will shape our tomorrow."

Melissa propped herself up with her elbows on the table and placed her chin in her palms; her eyes flickered with a mischievous glint.

"A businessman, a volunteer friend of nature and now a philosopher. I wonder if you have any other professions under your belt…"

Will blushed slightly. "I am talking incessantly. Sorry, it's not like me to talk so much and so pedantically."

Melissa reached out and touched Will's hand on the table. "Believe me, your conversation is as enlightening and relaxing as it is enjoyable." She quickly pulled back when she realised where her hand was; not knowing where else to put it, she began playing with the curls of her hair. Her gaze lingered on random things aimlessly. "For so long, I lived trivially within such a hurried whirl…" She continued after a deep sigh. "Coming here, this journey and what I learned about my father, all of these things were great opportunities for me to enhance my self-awareness, just as you said."

After a little silence, Will spoke with a narrow, intense gaze. "Well then, may I ask you a private question?"

Melissa returned his gaze with the same intensity. "Of course, what do you want to learn?"

"Who is waiting for you in America?"

She was happy at his question and didn't care to hide the satisfaction in her smile. Trying to suppress her excitement, she said, "There is my mum. If you're asking about a boyfriend, a fiancée or something like that, no. Not anymore. It ended shortly before I travelled here. What about you? Is there anyone you are with?"

"I've been alone for a while. I had a relationship that lasted for three years. I thought everything was going fine. However, just when I was getting ready to propose, she left me for a rich man with a stable career."

"I'm sorry, that must have been difficult."

Will reclined and combed his hair back with both hands. "In retrospect, I think it's good that it was over. We expected completely different things from life. She liked grandiosity as much as I liked simplicity. The contrasts between us made us more attracted to each other for a while, but in the end, it was too much to bear for both of us. One should always be able to share a common perspective with one's partner. They should at least be able to compromise."

Both were silent, running through their past relationships in their minds. Was it so difficult to find the right person? Where had they gone wrong? Who knows, maybe at a time and place most unexpected, someone would come around and please their souls. Maybe that someone was already around… Was it too early to feel the way they did…?

It was Melissa who broke the silence. "You have a very nice place here. What prompted you to part company with your father and to set up this place?"

Will folded his arms over his chest; he enjoyed the incoming question. "Hmm! A good question. Actually, I knew it would be easy to work with him. He is a kind, easy-going man. But I am a bit too free-spirited, I'd like to make my own decisions independently. Though he did propose to withdraw from the business and leave it to me entirely, I did not accept it."

Melissa listened intently, putting her hands together and resting her chin on top of them. "Why?"

Will leaned forward from the chair he was reclining on and put his arms on the table. "I had two reasons. First, the restaurant is deeply entwined with our familial history – it was run by our family for three generations. It has a soul to it that needs to be preserved. I would rather my business be a reflection of me."

When he fell silent, Melissa nodded, gesturing her understanding.

As he continued, Will's gaze softened with fellow feeling. "Secondly… If my father had quit working to give me space to be free, he would just be idle. Not having a direction or something to strive for is hard at any age, but it is much more difficult once you get older. Purposelessness consumes one's vigour of life. An endeavour that you love and are passionately attached to, which the restaurant is for my father, allows you to start each day afresh. I couldn't deprive him of that."

Melissa admired Will's determination, his kind-heartedness and the toughness of his spirit. She felt the gates of her heart open wide and her emotions warmly flow towards him; she didn't want to hold back.

As Will got up and poured another cup of coffee, he asked curiously, "What made you choose to be a veterinarian?"

Melissa spoke while adding milk to her coffee. "I love animals. My childhood dog Dodo had a big influence on my decision. On the day he died, when I was twelve, I decided to become a veterinarian. Since then, I have felt that I have this special bond with animals," she mused; her lips curled into a smile when she conjured up the image of Dodo in her head.

"I noticed your bond with animals the first time I saw you with Foam."

When Melissa turned her loving gaze to the dog lying on a soft cushion on the floor, she felt a certain unease. The animal was shaking slightly; it did not seem normal at all. Besides, it hadn't moved from its position in a long time. She got up from her chair with an anxious expression and knelt on the floor. Her eyes were closed as her hands inspected the dog's body. It was as if she was in a trance; she spoke with a barely audible voice. "Okay little one, no need to be afraid, everything will be fine. You are a very good, sweet dog; we love you." Her fingers lingered at a spot; when she pulled away the fur and laid the skin bare, she knew that the problem was right there. She turned to Will and showed him the wound she had discovered.

"Something scratched her deep, probably while we were in the wooded area, and then it got infected. But it is a simple ailment, it should quickly go away with some medication."

Will's strained expression loosened and relaxed. While he was caressing Foam, he turned towards Melissa standing very close him; his eyes, which had just grown grey with the coldness of sorrow, were once again sparkling blue with hope. "Thank you, you really are special."

Their breaths were intermingling as they stayed face to face, both kneeling near the dog with their legs and arms touching each other.

Melissa stood up nervously. "Nothing special, it is my job. Anyhow, I even started to consider myself as inadequate, seeing your devoted work here. When I go back, the first thing I'll do will be to participate in one of the programmes for wildlife conservation."

She asked for a pen and paper from Will, then wrote down the medicine that he needed to use. Peeking at the clock out of the corner of her eye, she noticed that they had spent quite a lot of time together. "I can't believe it! It's almost noon, I took up so much of your time."

She took her bag that she had hung on the back of the chair and headed for the door. Will reached her quickly and opened the door for her. "Good thing you were here. Without you, I wouldn't be able to understand what was wrong with Foam before it got worse. Besides, the time I spent with you is so meaningful and precious to me."

Melissa lifted an eyebrow as she tugged a strand of her ginger curls behind her ear. "For sure, not everyone can get the chance to hang out with a legendary lost princess after all." She winked, as Will laughed.

He leaned against the door frame with his hands in his pockets and asked with anticipation, "Dinner?"

"Let me check my appointments, hmm! Coincidentally, I seem to be free for the evening."

There was hesitancy in Will's voice. "It may be a bit noisy in here. We can eat at my house if you'd like."

The offer thrilled Melissa. She was crimson red as she said, "Okay." She turned quickly and walked away to hide her face. Her heart had set sail for new horizons and its path was beyond her control. She felt happy, despite questioning whether she was ready. It seemed so easy to relate to Will, especially when contrasting him with Ron's negativity. But the distance between them was a problem that she could not underestimate. It wasn't a distance that could be travelled back and forth so easily. Will had made it clear that he liked being here and that he did not consider living a different life. Whereas Melissa had a life of her own on the other side of the ocean. She had her job, her mother, the things she was used to…

Still, she didn't want to puzzle over these now. It wasn't like there was anything serious yet. Also, hadn't she decided to listen to her intuition more? Her intuition had guided her thusly for now. She was going to just wait and see what time would offer…

She took out the white sweater that her father had gifted her from among the few clothes she brought, then hugged it close to her chest as if she was hugging her father. She mused with a smile, "I trust your tastes." She first gathered her hair up, then she decided to let it down. Should she go for light or dark makeup? She was surprised to see that it was time to leave when she checked the clock. The seconds had drifted so much slower in the afternoon. When she looked at herself in the mirror for one last time, she comforted herself, saying, "No need to worry, he's not Ron and he likes you the way you are."

Will's house was at the end of a steep road and it had an amazing view of the sea from the front. The door to the left of the narrow entrance led to an open-plan kitchen and living room. Will took Melissa's jacket and hung it on the coat rack mounted on the wall; they sat down on the three-seater tan leather sofa in the living room. The bookcase that covered the wall opposite them was made of the same natural unpolished wood as the coffee table in the middle, and the shelves were brimming with books. The cleanliness of the place caught Melissa's attention as well as its pristine, masculine style.

"Ooo, you have a very orderly, well-kept house."

Will was proud. "I like being organised; it makes everything easier."

Melissa inevitably thought of Ron. She squirmed as she recalled his obsession with order, after silently wishing, *I hope he's not like that.* She reassured herself about the decision she'd made. *I will not think of these things tonight, I will just enjoy the moment.*

While Will poured some wine, Melissa was taking a look at his books and music albums.

"You can choose an album and put on some music for us."

"I don't know much about this." She stopped briefly, picking a random CD from the stack. "Let's see if I was able to pick something nice."

Will smiled as one of Chopin's nocturnes played softly. "It's in your genes apparently. You've chosen one of the best and found my favourite."

During the meal, they chatted about this and that. Melissa was surprised at how easy the conversation flowed with someone that she had met so recently.

After the dinner, they cleared the plates on the table; after insisting incessantly, Melissa managed to convince Will to let her help him with the dishes. After a while, the two were sitting on the cosy and soft armchairs, facing each other in a comfortable position, sipping on their wine. Melissa was startled with the ringing of her mobile phone. She was taken aback when she reached up and saw Ron's name on the screen; her face turned chalk-white. As she put the phone on mute, flipped it over and put it back, Will was staring at her anxiously.

"It's nothing important. It's just someone I didn't expect to get a call from, I'll talk with them later," she said.

Since an slightly anxious mood was already in the air, Will decided to open up the subject that had been on his mind for days.

"I don't want to upset you, but I wondered how you felt after finding out about your father. You looked very distressed that day. If you don't want to talk about it, I'll understand. I just thought you might like to share and lighten your burden—"

Melissa interrupted him before he could finish his sentence. Once again, her moss-green eyes were shaded with the darkness of gloom. "I didn't bring it up because I didn't want to tire you with my own problems, but actually I really need someone to talk to." She gathered her wild curls to one side with her hand and continued, "I'm so confused... I think your cool-headed perception may help me clear my mind a lot."

William bowed down as the dimples near his lips increased in their sweetness. "My cool-headed perception is at your service, lost princess."

Melissa was grateful to this kind, compassionate man who tried to comfort her with his jokes. For a while, she just swirled the wine in the glass, studying its movement.

"Do you think there is any logical explanation of what had happened to my dad? I mean, fairies and all that... I do think it is ridiculous, but at the same time, I cannot bring myself to altogether dismiss it. There are also dreams that I have been having every night since I arrived at Tobermory. Just like what the fairy told him; in my dreams my dad keeps telling me that I have special gift. I hope it's a harbinger of something good." Troubled, she looked at Will. She was afraid that he would think that she was crazy. "Ugh! I must be losing my mind. What was the name of that island where it all started?"

"Be easier on yourself, anyone in your place would be just as confused, but I'm sure that there is an explanation to all this. The name of that island is Staffa."

"There was something special about the place, wasn't there?"

"The Fingal's Cave, the cave mentioned in the story of your father, is famous for its acoustic features. In ancient times, they thought that it was a magical place; it was believed that the cave bestowed special abilities upon the musicians who went in there. This is all I know; we can check the internet and see if we can find any more information."

They spent the next hour searching the internet. Their research led them to the legends of the druids. The more information they gained, the more intriguing Bard's experiences began to seem, and her curiosity grew. As he was shutting down the computer, Will was excited by the idea that came into his mind.

"We should talk to Glenn, the librarian. I heard that she was especially interested in the druids. Besides, she is like a walking history book; she is very knowledgeable about historical events as well as recent happenings."

Melissa clapped her hands with joy; her face illuminated with excitement and her eyes shone like stars. "Fantastic! Then she may also know about my dad. When will we go meet with her then?"

Will felt like he was a moth to a flame. He straightened up, trying to keep his cool, jokingly took a peek at his watch and smiled. "I guess it's a bit late now – it can wait until tomorrow morning, right?"

Melissa tried to resist the temptation to reach out and kiss the dimples on his warm, loving face.

Glenn was a cheery and talkative grey-haired woman. She had been working as a librarian since she was young. She was fond of reading, so she loved her job. Will hugged her lovingly, then introduced her to Melissa. When she learned that Bard had passed away, her little round eyes were clouded in sadness. They had studied together in the same grade and she remembered him very dearly.

"I am very sorry, honey; I hope he had a good life. How did it go? Did he find fame there? He was very talented, everyone at school loved listening to him."

Melissa's heart dropped. "Unfortunately, no. He never pursued music."

Will knew that Glenn would ramble on about the matter, so he interrupted, sensing Melissa's apprehension. "You are the best person to enlighten us, Glenn. We are curious about the druids' beliefs, mystical abilities and secrets. I know that you are interested in these topics."

Glenn was delighted that they were consulting for her opinion; she straightened up. "You are right, I do have a special interest in druids. I can talk for hours and give you some encyclopaedic information if you want." She moved closer to them and continued with a low voice, as if passing on a secret, "But if what you are looking for is a deeper, more mystical, more psychic knowledge, I suggest you go to this man who claims to be a sage of druid descent."

Will furrowed his brows; he was baffled. "I've been living here since the day I was born and it's the first time I've ever heard of such a man."

"Most people don't know about him since he prefers to remain unnoticed. Anyway, there are no guarantees that you'll be able to meet him. He'll agree to meet you if he finds it appropriate." She picked up two books from the shelf and handed them to Melissa. "Let me know how it goes, okay?" she said, overwhelmed by her excitement, as she gave them the directions as to where to find the man and sent them off.

The sage's house was a makeshift wooden hut in a remote, secluded part of the oak forest, far outside the town. If you didn't know where to look, you would miss the little hut concealed amongst the threes. Melissa was already spellbound by this undertaking of which she had no interest or knowledge; however, with the eerie magical silence of the forest, her agitation peaked. If Will hadn't been with her, she would have never gathered the courage to journey to such isolated places of the isle and embark on such uncertain meetings. She seemed to be getting engulfed in a deep mystery. Were there actually such things as supernatural powers? Was that possible? Her knowledge of life until now told her that there were not. But what if…? When they got there, the sage greeted them at the door as if he'd known about their visit. He just stared at them without uttering a word, then turned and entered the hut, leaving the door open. Melissa and Will looked at each other, their eyes silently enquiring what to do. Will reached out and took Melissa's hand, quietly saying, "Let's go in." He squeezed her hand slightly as if to give her the strength to go on.

The sage, who was a scrawny man of medium height in his eighties, sat on the floor near the log fire in the middle and motioned for them to sit as well. His hair was completely white, with not a single black strand in sight, and it flowed down to cover his neck. The most unusual, striking feature of him was his eyes. His charcoal-black pupils were so large that the whites of his eyes were almost invisible. *They are like two bottomless wells*, Melissa mused. As the man stared unwaveringly, Melissa felt as if she was being pulled into a black hole. Her heart pounded in fear as she struggled to avert her eyes; she shuffled restlessly. Will once again took hold of her graceful hand, which he had let go of when they sat down, as if to say, "I'm here with you."

The sage spoke in a high and flat tone, without an expression on his face. "You don't have to be nervous. I'm just trying to connect with you and your ancestors. Now relax, don't avert your gaze."

Melissa intertwined her fingers with Will's, struggling to control her nervous, rapid breathing. "I'll try, but I must say, it's not easy."

When she plunged back into darkness of the sage's gaze, all sense of time and space was lost. Wandering through an infinite void, she was startled by the sage's voice and felt herself resurface at the speed of light. She had no idea how long she had spent in the void.

The man began to speak; his gaze was still focused on Melissa and his expression remained unchanged. "The ancestry of your grandmother goes back to the druidesses. She didn't have the gift; she was just a carrier. Fairies whispered the name of your father in his mother's ear; he was given the musical gift of the old bards."

For the briefest moment, a strange expression passed over his face. "There is also another gifted person in the family... It is you... You have been bestowed upon the power of healing. 'Melissa' is a medicinal herb with calming properties. Your ancestors have chosen the two of you for the continuation of their powers and rewarded you with these gifts."

Suddenly blood drained from Melissa's face; she turned white as a ghost. How did this man know all this? Was what she was hearing real or was she dreaming again? She was in shock and at the end of her wits; her brain was no longer able to process all that was happening.

The sage closed his eyes for a moment then opened them again, continuing his words. "Your father held the fairy responsible for the harrowing incidents and saw her as the source of his misery. However, all that had happened would have happened under any circumstance. His refusal or acceptance wouldn't have changed anything. The melodies of the fairy were to strengthen his soul, to shield it. These gifts can only be used if they are cherished and accepted. In other words, it is up to you to live up to your name; the choice is always yours."

When he was done speaking, the sage's pupils returned to their normal size. They knew that their visit had come to an end when the man stood up. As they left the hut, thanking him, they were both confused, not knowing what to think or say. What they'd heard was not something that one would hear every day; it was not easy to take in.

Melissa couldn't help but think what her father's life would have been like if he had accepted the gift. Would he have been happier? Could it be that ignoring his inherent gift and suppressing his creative nature had prepared an early grave for him? Although he did love his family, maybe he had never been completely happy. With such thoughts, Melissa decided to accept and explore her own gift of healing.

They did not speak on their way back; they didn't even look at each other. Withdrawn to their inner worlds, both were trying to comprehend, rationalise and make sense of it all. Melissa ruminated about the bond she had with animals and how easily she could connect with them. She relived how effortlessly she calmed down the animals that came to the clinic for her care, her experience with the stranded dolphin the other day, and her recent realisation of Foam's discomfort and early intervention. Did all those mean that the sage was right…?

Will finally broke the silence when they arrived at Tobermory. "Let's go to the pub. We need a drink."

"I think I'll need to drink all there is in the bar."

They tossed down the hard liquor that Will poured.

William was preparing the second shot when the alcohol loosened Melissa's tongue; sitting on the bar stool, she started to blabber on. "What do you think? Should we believe it, or do you think this guy is a fraud?"

"What would he gain by lying? He wasn't expecting anything from us."

"It cannot be a coincidence that he knew our names; he knew of my father, of his background, even his connection to music... everything."

Will put the shot glasses on the table and pointed at Melissa. "He also knew why we were there and the questions in our heads."

Melissa gulped down the second glass. She took her head in her hands. "Ugh! And what about all those things he said about me? I don't know what to think."

Will reached out, grabbed the graceful hand of Melissa resting on her ginger hair and pulled it near. He placed her hand in his palms and looked deep into her eyes.

"Let go of this deliberation and these thoughts about what needs to be done; just listen to your feelings, your intuitions; lend an ear to your inner voice – it will lead you to the truth." He paused, looking for hints of consent in her moss-green eyes to entice him. "Since the first time I ever saw you, I knew you were special. I believe the sage."

He reached out to the other side of the bar; his gaze shifted to her lips. He approached slowly and gave her a gentle kiss. Just when Melissa was questioning whether her heart could handle all the exhilaration, Will pulled back and said, "I'm sorry, I couldn't hold myself back."

In a split second, Melissa reached out and pulled him closer by his collar. "I'm sorry as well, because I liked it very much." Their lips met with passion. Melissa had to pull back when they were out of breath, worried that they would get overwhelmed by their emotion unless they stopped kissing.

"I think it's best if we stop now."

Will made every effort to slow down the beating of his heart. His misty eyes gazed at her with intensity.

~

After leaving Will's, Melissa walked for a long time to collect her thoughts. She had to look at these mysteries that were beyond her logic in a different light and re-evaluate things. She sat down on the wooden bench near the small stream flowing through the greenery. She took a deep breath, trying to soothe her soul, and whispered, closing her eyes with the memory of her father in her head. *I wish you could be here with me now. I need your advice. I could really use your help right about now.* The gentle splash of the flowing water, the harmonious rustling of leaves, branches swaying in the soft breeze, the chirping of birds; the meditative song of nature calmed her down. Feeling Bard's warmth enveloping her, she called out peacefully, "I wish you never gave up on music."

When she got back to her room, she went straight to snuggle under the duvet without even changing her clothes. As soon as she closed her eyes, Will's loving, caring, handsome face flashed in her mind. His lips were tender, his kisses seductive. As the thought of him charged all the cells in her body with desire, she muttered to herself, "Oh no! Am I falling in love?"

In her dream, she was in a cave that she had never seen or heard of before; Bard was coming towards her with open arms. When they met, they hugged and wept. Bard grabbed his daughter's face; his gaze reflected the pain and regret of all those years.

"My dear daughter, now you know what I've been through. I could not bear the burden of loss, I refused what was offered to me. Please don't repeat my mistakes – use the gift given to you. This is an opportunity for self-realisation, so do well out of it. Do not deny your nature." He kissed his daughter on the forehead. "I love you, Druidess…"

Still weeping, Melissa woke up with a jolt; she threw off the duvet and sat on the bed.

She called out to the void, "I love you too, Daddy." In that moment, the two of them were genuinely connected. Their conversation was real; the warmth of his kiss still lingered on her forehead. Who knows, maybe it really was possible to communicate with someone in a whole another dimension… Melissa's perspective was evolving. This way or that, what mattered was that her father was able to give her the answer she needed.

It was late, almost midnight, but she couldn't wait until morning; she was dying to call Will and tell him what she saw. She dialled the number before she could change her mind.

Will was surprised. Before he could ask anything, Melissa blurted out, "I'm sorry, I couldn't wait." She described her dream, then asked, "If possible, can we go to Staffa tomorrow to visit the Fingal's Cave?"

"Of course we can, I'll pick you up in the morning, but for now just take it easy and have a restful sleep. You need it, today was very tiring and hectic."

"Yes, thank you again for everything, goodnight."

"Goodnight, healer lost princess."

She was just putting the phone down when Will called out, "One more thing... I'm glad you called me to share it with me."

~

Will, who was waiting for her outside the hotel in the morning, felt his soul irradiating when Melissa walked out. Her red curls glowed and glinted like the sun. When their lips met, a volcano of heat erupted and warmed his whole body with its impact.

When they reached the pier, Will chartered a small boat for them. Melissa felt a little nervous, but Will's presence was reassuring. The unexpected serenity of the sea granted them a comfortable journey. Surprised with the stillness of the sea, the captain said, "Interesting, we are having one of those rare good days, you seem to be lucky." He docked the boat with ease and they made land.

As they were walking hand in hand towards the cave, Will paused for a moment, looked at her with tenderness and asked, "Here we are, where it all began. Are you ready?"

Melissa nodded, shaking like a leaf. "I am ready with all my being."

Chapter 18

THE TURQUOISE SEA IN BETWEEN THE DARK ROCKS CAST light upon the cave interior, its glow playfully reflected on the menacing cold rocks creating magnificent patterns of light. The echoes of the water were like an enchanting melody. Melissa sensed her father's presence. It almost felt as if he could appear out of nowhere and hug her like he had in her dream. Wishing from within the depths of her heart that her dream would come true, she looked around. Tears filled her eyes as she imagined the things young Bard had gone through here. As she was contemplating, *It's strange how the little things in life can set people on such different paths*, she heard Will's gentle voice: "I can leave you alone for a while, if that's what you'd like."

Melissa grabbed his arm with both of her hands; her vulnerable gaze pierced Will's soul. "No, no, please stay, I feel safe with you by my side."

Will put his hands on her face and gazed lovingly at her. "I'll stay as long as you want…"

As their lips interlocked, their souls were also united. At that moment, amongst the harmonious melodies of the cave, Melissa heard her father's voice and his song rising from the depths. In wonder, her eyes searched around, though she knew already that she was not going to see anything.

Will looked around nervously. "What happened? Did you hear something?"

Melissa's eyes sparkled; she smiled peacefully as tears rolled down her cheeks. "My dad knows I'm here and he accompanies us with his song."

"There is a very strong, special bond between the two of you. I am happy that you got to experience a love so great."

Melissa looked deep inside the cave and called out to the void, "I love you, Dad. Your soul is with us, I can feel it."

Will hugged her from behind; she closed her eyes, rested her head against his chest and, with her hands on the arms that were wrapped around her, listened to the melodies of the cave.

When they returned to Tobermory, Melissa wanted to go to the hotel and rest. She was tired both physically and emotionally. She gave Will a kiss as she got out of the car and assured him that she would call him as soon as she recovered her strength.

Walking absent-mindedly past the hotel door, Melissa was shocked to see who was sitting in the entrance hall. He jumped up as soon as he noticed Melissa and came running to hug her. Before she could say anything, he pressed his lips to Melissa's. He kissed her so longingly and embraced her so tightly that it was hard to raise an objection.

Meanwhile, behind them, Will rushed in to bring over the phone that Melissa had left in the car. His face grew chalk-white at the sight of the two in front of him. For a short moment in time, he did not know what to do, then turned back in haste as if he was running away and threw himself out. He was having trouble breathing. His heart was shattered with disappointment; it pained him deeply. He drove away as soon as he got in his car. He drove heedlessly. The warm lips that had kissed him just half an hour ago were now someone else's. They probably were never his anyway; she was probably just settling for a holiday fling. His thoughts made his blood boil and he twitched in anger. He parked at a secluded space by the sea and just sat in the car. He kept wondering when he'd fallen so deep in love, how he'd made the same mistake again. Yet, it did happen; he'd fallen in love and once again it had slipped from his fingers when he'd least expected it. He had lost it as quickly as he'd found it.

He got out, leaned against the bonnet of the vehicle and gazed at the sea with lightless eyes. For the past few days, his dreams of the future had always seemed to include Melissa. Now he had lost both her and his dreams.

No matter what, he wasn't going to bother her. She was already confused by her father's past and what she had learned about him; he was not going to cause any more distress for her; he had no right to do so. To love was to set free, to make sure they were happy, even if it meant his own unhappiness.

When he arrived at the pub, he passed to the back of the counter without greeting anyone, then took a pen and paper to scribble down a note explaining that he had to be away for a while. He gave the note to his assistant along with her phone, to be delivered to Melissa. Then, he went to the restaurant to see his father and briefly told him about what had happened. He avoided eye contact as much as possible, with despair weighing down his shoulders like a heavy burden.

"I have to get away. You'll keep an eye on the pub until I get back, right?"

Sean was upset with the way things had unfolded and that his son was left heartbroken. Both him and Cordelia had noticed the spark between the two young people and were delighted. The idea that his son could be with the daughter of his best friend was especially meaningful for Sean. Unfortunately, things do not always turn out as expected. The only thing he could do right now was help mend his son's broken heart.

"Don't you think about the pub now. Are you going to stay in the lodge?"

Will nodded.

"Let me know when you get there then." Sean put his hand on Will's shoulder and squeezed it. "Just keep us in the loop."

Sitting beside Melissa in front of the window in her room was Ron, who kept apologising and telling her how sorry he was for everything. He got down on his knees and took out the engagement ring, which Melissa had returned previously, out from his pocket. He reached out and took her hand.

"My life has been just unbearable. After you left, everything lost its meaning. I realised that I hurt you too much, that I was selfish. Please give me another chance."

He placed the ring on her finger when he was done speaking. Melissa was frozen; she was unable to respond. It was as if she was in a whole another dimension. Her head was in a spin. She thought of Will; what was it that she felt for him? She didn't even know him all that well yet. More importantly, what were his feelings for her? Not to mention, there was an ocean between the two of them, so how could it work out? Should she give it another try out of respect for what she used to have with Ron, or should she daringly leap into something brand new? Ron was a part of the life she knew, the life that she was used to, her real life in America. She was only here for a brief moment in time. Bewitched by the whimsy spell of her vacation, she had enjoyed the loving, amorous moments she'd had here; however, this was, after all, only a fairy tale and soon it was going to come to an end. She made her decision, thinking, *These tales have no place in reality!*

She was woken from her reverie by a knock on the door. It was Will's assistant, coming to deliver her phone along with the note. Upon receiving the note, Melissa quickly hid it away in her pocket.

Ron called out curiously. "Who was that?"

"Just someone delivering my phone. I had left it somewhere."

Averting Ron's eyes, she went straight to the bathroom, sat on the closed the lid of the toilet and unfolded the note with a slight shake of her hands; she then took a deep breath and read:

Dear Melissa,

I have to go away for something urgent. I believe I won't be back for a while. I cannot lie and say that I was not upset by what I saw when I walked in the hotel after you to give your phone. I guess you made up with your fiancé. I hope you'll be happy wherever you are and whoever you're with; never lose the sparkle in your eyes, the healer, the lost princess…

Melissa pressed the note to her chest and whispered as she cried, "Sorry, Will."

Ron snuggled up to Melissa and kept his arms around her all through the night. He told her about what had happened in his life while she had been away and how their acquaintances were doing. Whereas Melissa told him of about what she learned about her father, though she refrained from mentioning the fairies and the druids. She has also decided to keep her mixed emotions to herself, as she noticed that Ron's arrival had not stirred any excitement in her soul.

The next day, Melissa took Ron for a walk to show him around the town. He, too, was surprised by how calm and secluded the place was. Yet, there was no spark of delight or admiration in his eyes as he climbed up the hill and looked upon the scenery.

"Nice place to travel for a short vacation to wind down, but I don't think anyone can stay here for too long. I bet it vexes one's soul after a while. There is no social life, no entertainment, no movement; the life here is completely isolated," he snubbed.

Melissa did not share his opinion, yet she didn't bother to raise an objection. As she mused – *Well, it is a matter of preference, after all* – she let her thoughts wander within the winding paths of her mind for a second. Will's words rang in her ears: "The choices we make today shape our tomorrow."

She gathered herself then heard Ron's voice.

"Did I say something that bothers you?"

"No, no, I was just thinking that I am going to miss this place."

"What is there to miss? It's a barren countryside, there is no life here."

Melissa called Sean and informed him about Ron's arrival. They were planning to leave Tobermory tomorrow, that was why she wanted to meet today and bid them goodbye. They agreed to meet up at the restaurant in the evening.

Cordelia and Sean were sitting at the table near the window, waiting for her. They were heartbroken and even a little hurt. They couldn't help thinking, *If she was already engaged, why did she raise our son's hopes?* Still, they were kind enough to conceal their emotions. When Sean saw Melissa, he got up and called out to her. After ordering their food, they casually chatted about this and that. It was Cordelia who first tried to dispel the air of despondency shrouding their conversations. She took Melissa's hand in her palm and flashed her a cute, dimpled smile.

"We didn't think you'd be going so soon, we're sorry to see you leave."

Seeing the dimples in her smiling cheeks, Melissa felt a pang of grief; her eyes glazed over. She spoke with an overly defensive tone to her voice; it was as if she was also trying to convince herself of what she was saying. "I fulfilled my dad's request and found out about his past all thanks to you. I will be forever grateful to you for that. I really loved this place and I loved being with you, but I can't stay any longer. My mom is alone, and I do miss her a lot, not to mention I also have to go back to work."

Sean's beady blue eyes dulled with the gravity of his dejection. "Bard must be proud of you. Your happiness must be giving his spirit peace."

Melissa's eyes teared up. With an attempt to lighten the mood, which was heavy with sombre longing, Sean said, "Tell that fiancé of yours, though your father may not be here with us, I am here for you, and you bet I'll be there to give him a talking-to if I ever hear that he upsets you, even with the distance between us."

Cordelia glanced at her sadly. "I wish Will could be here to say goodbye to you."

Melissa hands clasped the napkin in her hands even more tightly; her shoulders tensed. With trouble, she forced a slightly hysterical smile. "That would have been great. I hope you can pass over to him my thanks and regards for his help."

Sean excused himself to make his way to the table near the cashier, then returned with a file that he took out from the drawers. He pulled out a large yellow envelope from the file and handed it to Melissa.

"This is yours. I almost forgot it existed before you arrived. Bard gave me these before he left; as it turns out I had unknowingly waited for you to come by and get them for years. These are his legacy and they should be yours."

She saw the papers filled with musical notes when she slightly lifted the end of the envelope open and peeked inside. Her eyes widened in surprise. She embraced the envelope close to her chest. "Are these his compositions?"

When Sean nodded yes, Melissa got up and hugged him, and after giving a big kiss on his cheek, she did the same to Cordelia. "I love you."

Cordelia sniffled as she smiled sweetly. Sean touched Melissa's shoulder. Ron's existence was forgotten or unimportant.

"You always have a family here waiting for you and thinking of you, don't you ever forget that."

As she was parting with these good-hearted people whom she'd bonded so closely with despite the short amount of time they'd had together, Melissa's tears fell down like raindrops.

"How could I ever forget? You guys are so important to me. I am sincerely thankful for each of you."

Chapter 19

On her first day back in Baltimore, she went to see her mother. When Judith opened the door, Melissa was once again welcomed by the homely scent of cinnamon that she loved. The lovely aroma always reminded her of home.

"I missed you and your cinnamon cookies."

Though it was a short separation, maybe due the fact that she had been so far away, Judith had missed her greatly. She teared up as she hugged her. "Me too, honey."

Sitting in their usual armchairs, nibbling on their cookies and sipping their teas, Melissa told her everything she had learned about Tobermory and the story of her father's past with all its details. Tears drifted silently over Judith's cheeks as she listened. The pain that the man she loved had suffered at such an early age, the remorse that burdened him, the wound that was inflicted on his soul grieved Judith deeply.

"I wish he had shared it with me, if I'd known, then maybe I could have brought him some solace and try to make him reconcile with the music that he loved so much. Maybe he thought I wouldn't believe in his unusual, supernatural experience. He shouldn't have, however, for I believed in his every word throughout our relationship."

Melissa took her mother's face in both of her hands and gazed lovingly into her eyes. "You already did your best to make him happy. You always supported him; he had a calm and happy life with you."

Judith smiled tenderly. "I loved him dearly."

"I know, he knew it as well." Melissa sighed and changed the subject. "And what do you think about the sage and what he said about me?"

"Your father and I both always thought that you were a special child, that you were different from the others. You radiated positivity and lit up the room wherever you were. It was as if you were on a mission to make everyone around you happy. Your connection with Dodo, you becoming a vet, and a very successful one at that, these all proved just how gifted you were. It doesn't matter whether there is a mysticality about it or not, the sage is right nonetheless: you truly are a healer."

As Melissa recounted her short-lived romance with Will, her eyes sparkled like the sun, but soon the clouds gathered and the light that was reflected slowly faded.

Judith was very perceptive; she realised the change in her daughter. "I took a liking to this boy without even seeing him."

She still believed that Ron was not the right guy for her daughter, but she knew that Melissa had to discover it for herself. It was not right to meddle, especially not now...

~~

Eight months had passed since her visit to Scotland. She had started sharing the same house with Ron once again. Their first days had passed like a honeymoon. Ron listened to Melissa, asked for her opinions, considered her wishes. Though they continued their nightly outings and attended to invitations, they also went on strolls out in nature, which was much more to Melissa's liking. She even almost convinced Ron to adopt a puppy at one point. Still, the feeling that something was missing always lingered; Melissa was never completely happy. She often caught herself thinking of Will.

She continued working at the Happy Paws clinic. After seeing under the conditions that the clinic operated under back in Tobermory, the comforts that they enjoyed here made her feel a bit guilty. Especially in the first few days after her return; she kept ruefully comparing her working conditions with those of Lucy.

There was something else that often troubled her mind. It felt as if she had departed from all her powers of healing as soon as she returned home. She was even more ordinary now than she'd been before her travels. She could not bond with animals as easily as before; it took more time for her to arrive at a diagnosis. She seemed to have left the reverie of her father back in Scotland as well, along with her powers of healing; he no longer appeared in her dreams. It was as if those days were never been. The spell was broken; the fairy tale was over.

But wasn't this exactly what she'd told herself when she accepted Ron's offer? She'd known that this would happen; wasn't it her who convinced herself that fairy tales were no longer a part of reality?

The busy pace of work, the daily rush swirled around her, taking her in, making the existence of any spirituality practically impossible.

Her life with Ron was full of different gatherings and events. On one of those nights, they were once again attending a cocktail party organised by the bank that Ron was working for; the senior management was also going to be in attendance. The average age of the guests was quite high. Women above the middle age were all in a race to show off in their over-the-top jewellery and teased-up and sprayed hair-dos. Melissa did not judge them, but it just wasn't her style and it seemed unnatural to her. She felt like an alien, silently pondering, *What even am I doing here?* It was her who looked unnatural in this crowd; she did not fit in with these people.

She leapt on the opportunity when she saw Ron alone for a brief moment. "I'm so bored," she said. "Can't we leave a little earlier?"

Ron squinted his eyes; the disappointment in his gaze was incriminating. "I need to stay, honey, maintaining good relations with these people is important for my career and my future, but you may leave if you want to."

Melissa just opened her mouth to speak when someone called Ron's name and he turned around to join the group of people just ahead of them.

Melissa grunted to herself. "Of course, Ron's career is above all else."

It was a Sunday. Melissa got up early and took a shower. Trekking was in the plans today, as it had been a long time since the last time that they'd gone for a walk in nature. Even the thought of it enlivened her. While she was making breakfast, energised with anticipation, the walks she'd gone on with Will came flooding into her mind. She felt an emptiness in her heart. She had been experiencing this quite frequently these days, 'the emptiness'...

Ron woke up and joined her. Melissa poured some coffee for both of them and sat opposite him; she was expecting some praise or some thanks for the breakfast she'd prepared diligently when Ron spoke with caution in his tone.

"Honey, you threw the towel down on the bathroom floor again! Can't you be a little more attentive?"

Melissa's face sank at his captiousness. She thought, *I'm trying to make him happy and this is what he notices from all that I've done!* She didn't feel like responding to his criticism.

Ron was neither aware of the light that gleamed within Melissa nor did he notice it fading. He was reading his newspaper as he ate. After sipping on his coffee, he lowered the newspaper covering his face and asked, "Is the machine broken? Why is the coffee cold?" Hearing this, Melissa felt blood recoil in her veins, her energy depleted.

If Will was sitting in front of her now, they wouldn't even have the time to eat in between their chatter and laughter. Not to mention, he would catch the slightest change in her gaze and would try to make her feel better. Melissa missed his warmth and the feeling of safety she felt near him. She was no longer able to contain the emotions and thoughts she had long suppressed.

After breakfast, when Ron left saying that he had to work for the day, Melissa realised that she was relieved that their plans had fallen through. *What am I doing?* she asked herself. She had returned to the shallow routine of the life she'd had, disregarding her true desires, her goals and, most importantly, the core of her essence.

She wandered around every corner of their house weighing her feelings. It was no different from what she had felt when she'd left last year. She remembered what Will had said: "I think it is a way of self-expression, you know, how one styles the place where one lives. I think it is very personal; you can't call somebody else's creation yours." With regret, she realised that there wasn't even the slightest trace of her presence in this house.

She wanted to be herself, to live her life. She was whatever she was, nothing more, nothing less. She was tired of pretending and masking who she really was. She had to live her life plain, simple and honest. She wanted peace, but it could only be possible if the quarrel within her was over; it could only be possible if she loved and accepted herself. This resolution came as a surprise. Didn't she love herself? Why did she feel that way? Her family loved and valued her very much. Recently, she'd read in a book that people's traumas are sometimes passed on to them from their elders. The hurt would be rooted in our parents or our grandparents, and it would be carried on through their genes, causing emotions that one cannot thoroughly trace. Could that be why she was never truly happy? Was she perpetuating the punishment that her father imposed on himself? Was she afraid to live her life to the fullest? Still, the book described that the chains of such vicious cycles could be broken with awareness and conscious decisions. By that, she could bring peace both to herself and to her father. Yet, it was not possible to do this if she was with Ron.

She took a blank paper and a pen, then sat down at the table where they had just eaten breakfast.

Dear Ron,

You are a good, honest man; you are true to your nature. Whereas I tried to be someone who I never was but always thought I should be. I apologise. No matter how hard a person tries, their essence does not change; they can pretend for only so long. But we shouldn't have to pretend to begin with, right? We either have to accept our loved ones as they are or let them go and set them free. You and I see life from two very different perspectives; you are also well aware of that. I'm sure that there is someone out there who can make you happy, who has similar views on and expectations of life as you do, but unfortunately that someone is not me. I no longer want to be dishonest, both to you and to myself. I gave it another try but it didn't work. I hope you find the happiness you deserve. Goodbye.

With love,
Melissa

Melissa moved in with her mother until she found herself a new home. Although Judith insisted that she could stay with her, Melissa wanted to set her own way. Her own house, furnished with the things she'd chosen for herself... The place she lived should reflect who she was. She didn't have to wait too long before she happened to find the place she was looking for, just two blocks from Judith's house.

There was a massive oak tree in front of the French balcony of the small and cosy one-bedroom apartment on the fourth floor. She had already warmed up to the well-kept and clean apartment, but it was the spectacular tree that reassured her and made her decision certain.

She furnished the house with care and she was very satisfied with everything in the end. Still, there was something missing. Something that could lift her spirits, something that would fasten her grasp on life and happiness.

She found what she was looking for in an animal shelter she visited. She felt an instant fondness the moment she saw the round eyes of the little pug beaming from its jet-black fur. The puppy reminded her of Foam. It was almost as if the puppy was also saying to her, "Please pick me," as it jumped into her lap and licked her face. She dropped by her mother as she took it back home. When Judith saw the cute dog, "Goodness!" she exclaimed. "It's as black as charcoal." With that Melissa found out what to name the puppy: 'Coal'.

Melissa's life was moving in the direction she wanted. Living in her own home with Coal was delightful; she spent more time in nature and had the freedom to do whatever she wished to do. The only problem was the longing she felt deep in her soul. She missed Will and his dimpled smile. If only she had known then what she knew now, she would have never left him there and come back, but it was too late now, she had already broken his heart.

Melissa had returned from a walk; she had just washed Coal and was now combing its fur. Hearing the phone ring, she put the dog down and got up to answer. The caller was an official from a music production company and she was being called for a meeting. It took some time for Melissa to get over her astonishment and grasp what was going on. She had sent Bard's compositions, which she had received from Sean, to a music producer, to ask for a professional opinion. It had been five or six months, maybe even more, and she'd completely forgotten she had even sent them.

She attended the meeting with Judith. After the secretary informed the person waiting for their arrival, a man walked out from his office to greet them outside. He was extremely respectful and paid great heed to his two guests. Melissa and Judith exchanged confused glances. They were not expecting such a zealous welcome; in fact, they did not really know what to expect. When they settled in the stylish leather armchairs in the office, an assistant served them champagne. They felt like famous artists.

The man waited for them to sip their drinks for a little while, then he broached the subject. "These compositions you've sent to us." He was holding the papers of musical notes as he spoke. "These are wonderful! It has been a long time since I've heard such refined, soulful music. Bard McLoyd had a rare, special talent. I truly wish he were with us, for it would have been an honour to meet him."

Melissa and Judith's expressions were full of pride, as two pairs of moss-green eyes sparkled with tears. In shock, their pupils grew into large and shiny emerald stones when they heard the figure that the man offered to them. This was incredible. They'd never expected anything like this. While they were willing to accept the offer, the only request they made was that they wanted the album to be titled *Whispers of a Fairy*.

These musical compositions were the fairy's gift to Bard, and Bard's gift to them... Bard's soul was going to live on as his music resounded, making him eternal.

With some of the earnings from the album, Melissa wanted to help the clinic in Tobermory, which was on the brink of closing down. With that in mind, she contacted Sean. She hadn't known the name of the foundation that sponsored the clinic, and she was stunned when she found out. 'Maidie McPearson'. The foundation had been established by her father, Ewin, who named it after her.

All this could not have been a coincidence. The system and the structure of life operated mysteriously and inexplicably. Bard was paying his dues somehow; he reunited with his Maidie and he brought his beloved daughter and wife together with the people who had also been very dear to him.

All the paperwork for donation were made under great confidentiality, with Sean's support.

Melissa and Judith jointly decided to change the name of the foundation.

WHISPERS OF A FAIRY
Maidie McPearson and Bard McLoyd Wildlife Support
and Conservation Foundation

At this time, Melissa urged her mother to travel with her to Scotland. In fact, she didn't have to insist too much since Judith already knew that her daughter's mind and heart were enthralled by what was there. She wanted to get to know this Will, whom Melissa had told her about. She was also thrilled by the idea that she could feel closer to Bard upon seeing the places he had been born and raised.

Melissa's only fear was that Will might have found someone else. When she hesitantly enquired with Sean about this, she was relieved by the reply she received.

As they made their way to the airport, Melissa was thinking about her visit last year. The change she'd gone through was so great that it felt like it had been centuries, but her emotions were just as warm as if it was only yesterday. She didn't know what to expect when she set out for her previous trip, whereas now, she knew that she could find love, peace and trust there.

Judith thought that her daughter was glowing, and she was happy to see her like that. She had never lost faith that Melissa would eventually make the right choice.

By the time they arrived in Tobermory, it was almost evening. They settled in their rooms at the hotel. Judith was exhausted; she was feeling the jet lag as well, so she took a shower and went straight to bed. Coal was still under the influence of the sedatives he'd been given for the flight. Melissa, however, could hardly contain her excitement. She was finally here… She wanted to see Will as soon as possible.

There was a soft hail outside. Will was going to close up the pub early and meet with his family for Christmas dinner. When the last table cleared, he dismissed his assistant, sat alone in front of the fireplace and contemplated. All of a sudden, Foam, who was sleepily curled up near Will's feet, pricked his ears up and began to bark; he shot up like an arrow towards the door as he heard it open.

Walking through the door, Melissa greeted Foam with open arms. The dog licked her face with wild excitement as Melissa chuckled and laughed. "Hey! Take it slow. Okay, okay, I missed you too."

Will gaped at the sight, wide-eyed. He got up from his seat and walked towards the moss-green depths of her eyes, unblinking as he was worried that she would disappear.

Melissa bit her lip as she tucked the crimson curl on her cheek behind her ear. "Would you buy a drink for a guest who has returned to her father's homeland after being lost and adrift in a faraway land, only to realise that here is where she belongs?"

Will's eyes glowed. "Well, if she is the lost healer princess of the mysterious king…" He held Melissa's face lightly; just before placing a kiss on her lips he asked, "Is there a special reason why the princess wanted to be here?"

Melissa glanced, anxiously pondering, *Am I too late?* She answered, "She thinks she has found her soulmate here and wonders if he feels the same…"

It was as if both of them were in a trance. The concept of time and space perished as they just sensed each other's presence; their souls flowed into each other through their gaze.

Will hugged her waist with one hand, and with the other, he slowly lifted her chin, raising her face to his own. Before kissing her gingerly, he whispered, "I thought you would never come back. I've been so miserable since you've been gone…"

"I had to go for a while in order to be able to come back here with reassurance." The green of Melissa's eyes was like the depths of the forest: consuming, bewitching and inviting. "It took some time, but now I'm certain. I feel at home next to you, I know that now."

"My dear princess, I love you so much."

When their lips met with desire once again, Melissa heard Bard's voice coming from deep within her.

"Welcome home, Druidess."